By the bestselling authors of **Specky Magee**,
Specky Magee and the Great Footy Contest,
Specky Magee and the Season of Champions
and **Specky Magee and the Boots of Glory**.

www.speckymagee.com

PUFFIN BOOKS

Published by the Penguin Group
Penguin Group (Australia)
250 Camberwell Road, Camberwell, Victoria 3124, Australia
(a division of Pearson Australia Group Pty Ltd)
Penguin Group (USA)
375 Hudson Street, New York, New York 10014, USA
Penguin Group (Canada)
90 Eglinton Avenue East, Suite 700, Toronto, ON M4P 2Y3, Canada
(a division of Pearson Penguin Canada Inc.)
Penguin Books Ltd
80 Strand, London WC2R 0RL, England
Penguin Ireland
25 St Stephen's Green, Dublin 2, Ireland
(a division of Penguin Books Ltd)
Penguin Books India Pvt Ltd
11 Community Centre, Panchsheel Park, New Delhi – 110 017, India
Penguin Group (NZ)
Cnr Airborne and Rosedale Roads, Albany, Auckland, New Zealand
(a division of Pearson New Zealand Ltd)
Penguin Books (South Africa) (Pty) Ltd
24 Sturdee Avenue, Rosebank, Johannesburg 2196, South Africa

Penguin Books Ltd, Registered Offices: 80 Strand, London WC2R 0RL, England

First published by Penguin Group (Australia)
a division of Pearson Australia Group Pty Ltd, 2006

10 9 8 7 6 5 4 3 2 1

Text copyright © Red Wolf Entertainment Pty Ltd and Gamel Sports
Media Pty Ltd, 2006

The moral right of the authors has been asserted

Designed by John Canty and Brad Maxwell © Penguin Group (Australia)
Cover photograph by Tim De Neefe
Typeset in 12/18 New Baskerville by Post Pre-press Group, Brisbane, Queensland
Printed and bound in Australia by McPherson's Printing Group,
Maryborough, Victoria
Colour separation by Splitting Image

National Library of Australia
Cataloguing-in-Publication data:

Arena, Felice.
Specky Magee and a Legend in the Making.

ISBN 0 14 330189 6.

1. Australian football – Juvenile fiction. I. Lyon, Garry, 1967– . II. Title.

A823.3

www.puffin.com.au

Specky Magee
& a legend in the making

Felice Arena &
Garry Lyon

Puffin Books

G'day, all!

Well, here it is . . . the next mega-action-packed Specky adventure.

If you've read all four previous Specky books it's great to have you back! If this is the first time you've picked up a Specky novel, then welcome – and don't worry that you haven't read the others yet, you can always check them out later.

Since writing the series many people have asked me what it's like knowing a real live legend of Australian Rules Football. And I usually answer, 'Well, I've only met Eddie McGuire a couple of times and . . . oh . . . you meant my old school mate Garry Lyon? Oh, yeah, he's all right. He still hasn't admitted that I took an awesome 'specky' over the top of him back in primary school . . . but, yeah, he's okay.'

But seriously, the one thing that all legends possess is passion. And Garry has bucket-loads of it. He's passionate about whatever he puts his mind to. Footy, writing . . . And that's what makes it brilliant working with Garry.

In this latest novel a few people will find that their passion is tested as they're torn between the things they love. So if you have a passion for something (you might even have a few), then my advice is be the best you can be and go for it! You might become a legend along the way.

Cheers!

Felice

Hey there!

I can't believe that we're up to the fifth Specky Magee adventure already. It seems like only yesterday that Felice approached me with an idea to write a story about a young boy with a love for footy and a dream to play in the AFL one day.

Well, as you will discover, Specky continues to take small steps to make that dream a reality. It's not always easy, though, and he continues to confront new hurdles along the way. But in doing so he begins to understand that not all people share the same goals and ambitions, and that what is important to one person is not necessarily important to another. Life is all about respect: respecting your family, your friends, your teachers, your coaches and, yes, even your adversaries.

As you may know, Felice and I grew up in the same country town. We both ended up here, in Melbourne, but for entirely different reasons. While football took me away from home, Felice pursued a career in acting. He turned that into a very successful career, and it eventually took him around the world. While you now recognise him as a famous author, I respect him enormously for following his heart and taking a chance on what he was passionate about.

Now an old footballer and an old actor are writing kids books together. Who would have thought?! It led to the first Specky Magee book and, now, to *Specky Magee and a Legend in the Making*. I'm pretty happy about that. Hope you are too.

Enjoy

Garry

1. derek 'screamer' johnson

'Derek!' growled Mr Johnson from his armchair. 'While you're there, get me another one, will ya?'

Screamer shuffled into the lounge room and handed his dad a can of beer.

'Can you believe this joker?' Mr Johnson continued, pointing at the TV.

Screamer looked over at the screen as he dropped onto the couch in the corner of the room. He and his dad were watching *Sensational Stuff*, the most popular footy show in the country.

'I can't believe the clowns they have on this program – going on about how much the umpires need stress-free weekends away, and how the league should pay for it. What a load of bull!'

Screamer watched his dad swig a huge gulp from his can, then belch loudly.

'Don't tell me! Look who they've just brought out on the panel. It's bloody Michael Michaels. Craig used to call him Mickey Mick. Hell! The kid's made the big time.'

Screamer's dad shook his head sadly.

'You all right?' Screamer asked.

'Yeah, I'm fine,' his dad snapped, looking back up at the telly.

Screamer knew he wasn't.

'Bloody Mickey Mick,' Mr Johnson mumbled again. 'AFL's newest young-gun player talking to Teddy McMahon on *Sensational Stuff*. He was your brother's rival, you know that?'

Screamer nodded, suddenly feeling anxious. He didn't want to talk about his brother, Craig.

'He and Craig used to have some tough battles at school. They both fought to play in the same position – like you and Magee last year. By the way, did he turn up for training this arvo?'

'Nup,' answered Screamer, hoping his dad would get the hint that he wasn't in the mood to talk.

'So, the great Simon "Specky" Magee finally got the hint, did he?'

'Yep – when we told him on Tuesday night we didn't want him on the team anymore.'

'Good on ya, lad! I'm glad you convinced those mates of his – that Roberts kid . . .'

'Robbo,' corrected Screamer, rolling his eyes.

'Yeah, Robbo, and that little Italian rover, Castoni . . .'

'Castellino. Danny Castellino.'

'Yeah, him, and the speedy Indian lad and the kid who commentates everything, and that geeky, brainy one . . .'

'The Bombay Bullet, Gobba, and Einstein,' corrected Screamer again, annoyed that his dad couldn't be bothered getting his teammates' names right.

'Yeah, well, all of 'em. They owe you for setting them straight about Magee. Well done.'

Screamer was surprised. Had his dad just said something nice about him? Screamer grinned proudly. It was rare for him to get a compliment from his father.

Mr Johnson finished off the rest of his beer. And burped again.

'Serves Magee bloody right, ya know. Blowing it with a great footy school like Gosmore Grammar.

What an absolute idiot. Only idiots get themselves expelled from school.'

'I was expelled,' said Screamer, his moment of pride suddenly over. 'From Ridley, remember? That's why I'm at Booyong High.'

An awkward pause followed. Then the telephone rang.

Mr Johnson picked up the hand-held from the coffee table.

'Hello?'

'Derek?' Screamer's mum appeared at the door and motioned him to join her in the kitchen. Screamer left his father to take the call.

'Yeah?' he said.

Even at fourteen, Screamer towered over his mother. She reached up to ruffle his hair.

'He mentioned Craig, didn't he?' she asked.

Screamer brushed her hand aside.

'Yeah, like about a hundred times in the last hour,' he replied flatly, opening the fridge door.

'Well, it is his birthday next week.' His mum paused, then said quietly, 'I went to visit Craig today, you know.'

Screamer slammed the refrigerator shut. He

settled for an apple from a bowl on the kitchen table.

'Did you hear me?'

'Yeah, I heard you,' mumbled Screamer.

'So?'

'So, what?' Screamer shrugged his shoulders as he chomped into his apple.

'Maybe we can stop by to see him after –'

'What d'ya mean, see him?' Screamer said angrily.

'Derek, please . . .'

Screamer looked away from his mum and continued to bite at his apple.

'Fine, then,' she said, after a pause. 'If you're going to act like that, maybe I shouldn't tell you about my chat with Mr Li this afternoon.'

'What? When?' Screamer's tone had suddenly changed.

'Now you want to talk to me all of a sudden!' said Mrs Johnson, pulling a face.

'Come on! What'd he say?'

'Well, he said that you're definitely ready to go on to the next level.'

'Seriously?'

'Yes, seriously. He said on Sunday he wants to talk about something that might interest you.'

5

'What?'

'He wouldn't say. He said he'd tell us when we see him.'

'Cool! Anything else?'

'Well, not really – he's still asking me if I want to pay every six months rather than every week. I don't know why he keeps asking me – I've been paying him this way for the past four years. He knows your father will find out if I pay a lump-sum fee and –'

'Fee for what?' said Mr Johnson, walking into the kitchen.

'N-n-nothing,' stuttered Screamer's mum.

'Who was on the phone?' asked Screamer, quickly changing the subject.

'Can you believe it? It was your coach – if she can call herself that! *Coach* Pate.'

As Mr Johnson brushed past Screamer to grab another can of beer from the fridge, the phone rang again.

'I'll get that,' said Mrs Johnson, hurriedly leaving the room.

'So what did Coach Pate want?' Screamer waited as his dad shook his head, popped the can and took a gulp before answering.

'She had the nerve to call me to see if I could talk to you about your influence on your team-mates – and to find out how they've reacted to Magee's return.'

'What d'ya say?' asked Screamer.

'I told her to mind her own bloody business!'

'Derek, it's for you.'

Screamer's mum returned with the phone in her hand.

'Who is it?' asked Screamer. He rarely got calls.

'It's Christina.'

2. booyong high life

'Oh, terrific! Now the whole school knows why I'm back,' Specky said under his breath, embarrassed.

Specky was seated next to his good mate Johnny Cockatoo at the back of the classroom. There were only five minutes of English class to go before the lunchtime bell.

'What?' Johnny asked.

'This!'

Specky was reading an article in his school's newspaper, *The Booyong High Bugle*.

He shoved the paper across the desk, so that Johnny could read it.

HOW SPECKY-TACULAR IS YEAR 9 FOOTY CHAMP?

It was only last month that former Booyong High student Simon 'Specky' Magee led the Gosmore Grammar Knights to victory against our courageous Lions (and Magee's former teammates) in a thrilling Diadora Cup elimination match.

But now he's back!

Four days ago the Year 9 football champion, who had left us to take up a sporting scholarship at the private college, returned to Booyong after being expelled (something about 'borrowing' a pair of prestigious old boots).

Well, we at *The Bugle* would like to welcome Simon back, but now we can't help but wonder just how 'Specky-tacular' Magee really is.

Specky re-read the last line of the article out loud in a whiny, sarcastic voice.

'But now we can't help but wonder just how "Specky-tacular" Magee really is.'

'I wouldn't worry about it. They're just trying

to hook in more readers.' Johnny shrugged.

Specky had had a bit of exposure to the media in the last few years. There had been a couple of small mentions in the local paper about his football exploits, and the school-league scores and best-player lists were printed in the paper on Monday mornings. Every week, the first thing Specky did was to check whether or not he was featured. It wasn't that he had a big head or anything – Specky never once bragged about the fact that he was almost always named in the best two or three players – but he couldn't help getting excited about the recognition.

This article in *The Bugle*, though, was something new altogether. It was the first time that something had been written about him that was anything other than positive. If anyone had been in any doubt about what happened at Gosmore Grammar, then they sure knew the truth now.

'It happens to the best of 'em, Speck,' continued Johnny. 'Jason Akermanis always has stuff written about him, and not all of it is good. If your footy career keeps going the way it is, you better get used to it, man. The biggest stars in the AFL can't even let one rip without making it onto the back pages. Maybe I could be your publicity officer. I can just see it now . . . *Mr Magee has no further comment to make on this matter and he would appreciate it if you respected his privacy.'*

Specky mustered half a grin.

'And besides, they have nothing else to write about,' added Johnny.

'Yeah, I s'pose,' nodded Specky, notching it up as just one more weird thing to add to one of the weirdest weeks of his life.

He couldn't believe that on Monday he had been a student at Gosmore and now, midday Friday, he was back at his old school. And to make it even more surreal, life at Booyong High was very different from the way it had been when he left it.

'Specky, man?'

'Hmm?' said Specky, looking back up at Johnny.

'What are you thinking?'

'What?'

'I said, I'll be able to play again next week. The doctor said my injury has healed nicely, and you didn't say anything.'

'Oh, sorry, mate. I was just thinking how

bizarre everything is, you know, with you living in Melbourne and Tiger Girl back from overseas and in our year. It's cool, but . . .'

Specky looked to the front of the classroom to see Danny, Robbo and Screamer sitting together.

'But Danny and Robbo are acting like total knobheads and giving you the silent treatment – which isn't cool,' added Johnny, finishing Specky's sentence.

'Yeah, that,' mumbled Specky, as Screamer turned around and sneered at him.

'Well, stuff 'em! That's what I reckon. If any-one should be giving you a hard time, it's me. I'm the one you cleaned up – that broken collar-bone put me out for six weeks.'

Specky nodded in agreement. Johnny continued.

'And they're just idiots if they believe that you thought you were better than them. It's only because Screamer's been baiting them like barramundi to a croc!'

Specky smiled again. He liked the way Johnny worded things, and he could tell that his friend was still adjusting to his new surroundings –

Booyong High was a million miles away from his beloved Outback.

'Yeah, I know,' replied Specky.

'And one more thing,' added Johnny in a loud whisper.

Both boys noticed that their teacher was staring in their direction. They were supposed to be working quietly on a review of a book or newspaper article.

'If I were you, I'd turn up tomorrow and play. Who cares what the team thinks? Coach Pate would put you in, in a second.'

'Nah, that would be too weird. Besides, I don't wanna be somewhere I'm not wanted,' Specky whispered back, just as the bell sounded.

Specky's classmates hurriedly packed up and shuffled out of the room. Specky and Johnny were the last ones to leave and join the chaotic stream of students in the corridors.

'But footy's your life. What are you gonna do?' Johnny said, raising his voice and trying to keep up with Specky in the lunchtime rush.

Specky heard Johnny, but didn't know how to answer him. He had asked himself that question over and over all week. And he didn't have an answer – just some vague idea about maybe checking out the local footy clubs. Specky promised himself he would just concentrate on getting through the next couple of days before making any definite decisions.

'Hey, Speck!'

Specky had almost walked past the Year 12 common room when he noticed his sister's boyfriend, Dieter McCarthy, motioning him over. Specky told Johnny he'd catch up with him outside where they usually had their lunch.

'Hey, Legend, I need your help,' said the Great McCarthy, pulling Specky inside.

Specky felt a little uncomfortable about being in the room the senior students of the school called their own. It was a huge area decked out with couches, a TV, stereo, and even a small kitchen.

'What's up?' asked Specky, noticing that some Year 12s were glaring at him.

'Well, there's two things – this week's footy tips, and your sister.'

'Yeah?' said Specky, wondering how those two things were connected.

'Help me with my picks,' asked Dieter. 'I was

leading the Year Twelve tipping comp until I stuffed it up last round. I need your thoughts on this weekend's games.'

'What's that got to do with Alice?' asked Specky.

'Nothing. I'll get to that in a sec. So, come on, what are your picks? You know all the AFL teams better than anyone else.'

As a rule, Specky prided himself on keeping up with everything that was happening in the world of football. He read the sports pages every day, devouring every snippet of football news that he could possibly find. He also walked around the house with his headphones on, listening to the various sports shows on the radio, following all of the debates that raged after a weekend of football. He loved listening to the opinions of the commentators, former players and journalists and had, occasionally, even called the talkback number to ask a question or two. Specky had been successful in lobbying his dad to get pay TV installed so he could keep up-to-date with the latest selection and injury news. It had also caused a few fights with his sister, Alice. When Alice's all-time favourite reality show clashed with *Footy Yak from My*

Armchair, a footy chat show with former AFL legend Bernard Sealy and the newspaper journalist Michael Heanan, all hell broke loose in the Magee household. Specky eventually had to strike a bargain with his sister to take the bins out AND pack the dishwasher, just so he could catch the first segment every week. In addition to all of that, Specky surfed the club websites every week to try and pick up some of the 'inside mail' that the other media might have missed. It all added up to the most amazing knowledge of the AFL and Dieter was aware that what Specky didn't know about football wasn't worth knowing.

'Well . . . Brisbane versus West Coast at the Gabba – I would normally take Brisbane at home, but I'd say go for West Coast. They're playing well with a full list, and their midfield has taken over from the Lions as the best midfield in the competition. Plus, the Lions' injury list is getting worse by the minute,' said Specky.

For the next few minutes Specky helped pick the rest of Dieter's tips for the round.

'And one more,' prompted the Great McCarthy. 'Richmond versus the Ds on Sunday.'

'You'd know that one better than me,' said

Specky, knowing that Dieter was a diehard Richmond fan.

'Yeah, you're right. I'll forget the whole *go with your head not your heart* thing. I'm going for my Tiges.'

'So, look who it is – my main man, the subject of my article.'

Specky stepped aside as a Year 12 girl pushed herself past him and Dieter.

'Main man? What?' Specky asked, confused.

'No hard feelings about the article?' asked the girl, smiling smugly as she made her way into the kitchen.

'Keep movin', Full On,' snapped Dieter, annoyed by the interruption.

Suddenly Specky realised who she was.

'Full On?' Specky questioned.

'Yeah, Theresa Fallon – everyone calls her "Full On". 'Cause she *is* most of the time.'

'She got stuck into me in her article –'

'Yeah, well, I wouldn't worry about her,' said Dieter, cutting Specky off mid-sentence. 'She thinks she's gonna be the next gossip column-ist for *TV Week* or a mega-newspaper tycoon or something. And she probably will be. She's obsessed with the paper. Now, about Alice.'

Specky filed the name 'Theresa Fallon' away as someone he needed to be a little careful around. He had read enough newspapers to know that the best journalists in the country never missed anything and that they could be ruthless when they were chasing down a story. It seemed that Theresa Fallon had ambitions of her own, and if a story emerged that involved Specky, good or bad, then she would have no hesitation in writing it.

Specky was feeling increasingly uncomfortable – more Year 12s were giving him dirty looks as they streamed into the room for their lunch.

'Has your sister mentioned anything about the deb to you?'

'The what?'

'Her debutante.'

'Her what?'

Specky realised he had been so caught up in his own life in the past week, he had no idea what was happening with Alice.

'Yeah, she's going to be a debutante. You know, where girls are presented to society at a ball. Make their debut. Really get dressed up for it, in white dresses and stuff.'

Specky noticed some panic in the Great

McCarthy's voice. He even seemed to have broken out in a cold sweat.

'What's that got to do with me? And why are you freaking out all of a sudden?' asked Specky.

'I'm not freaking out! It's just that each debutante asks someone to partner her at the ball. Then they have to do weeks of ballroom dancing practice and then at the ball they have to dance in front of their families and friends.'

Dieter was chewing his bottom lip nervously.

'So?' Specky said. 'What's the big deal? You're Alice's boyfriend. *You* should partner her.'

'I know, I know. But I can't.'

'Why not?'

''Cause I can't dance for nuts! I reckon I have a phobia about performing in front of others.'

'What?' Specky choked in disbelief. 'You used to be the mascot for the Richmond Footy Club. In front of thousands of people.'

'I know, but that's different – I was hidden in a costume. No one could see me. So, what I want you to do is let your sister know that maybe she should look for another partner.'

Specky couldn't believe what he was hearing. Dieter was supposed to be the Great McCarthy.

At the moment he was sounding more like the Great McChicken.

'Mate, haven't you seen that dancing show on TV? They have actors, swimmers, newsreaders, even AFL players doing all sorts of dances. Some of them are hopeless as, but they don't care! If they can do it, you can.'

Dieter sighed heavily.

'Don't you like Alice anymore?' Specky had to ask. 'Are you dumping her?'

'No! No! I really like her. I just can't dance.'

'So what? Don't be a wimp. Just do it!'

For a moment, Specky wondered if he had gone too far by calling Dieter a wimp. He looked pretty cheesed off.

Then he nodded. 'Yeah, you're right,' he agreed. 'I just have to grit my teeth and do it. Thanks, Speck.'

Specky rushed out of the common room to meet up with Johnny. He was only a few paces past the door when he was stopped again. It was Tiger Girl.

'Hey,' she said, swinging her arm affectionately around Specky's shoulders.

'Hi, TG,' smiled Specky.

'I wanna ask you something.'

First Dieter and now you, thought Specky. If it keeps going like this, lunchtime will be over before I know it.

'Okay, shoot!'

'Well, um –'

Suddenly Tiger Girl was interrupted by a Year 7 student barging in between them.

'Are you Simon Magee?' he asked, out of breath, looking up at Specky.

Specky nodded.

'Um, I just overheard Coach Pate talking on the phone with your mum in the staff room. And she said your dog just died. She's coming to tell you now.'

'What?' Specky asked, not believing what he had just heard.

The boy repeated himself.

Specky was lost for words. No way, he thought. This *can't* be happening to me! This is the worst week of my entire life.

Specky looked up to see Coach Pate heading his way.

'Are you sure?' Specky stuttered, feeling his chest tighten.

'Yeah, your dog's dead,' blurted the Year 7 kid.

Specky bolted off without bothering to wait for Coach Pate. He shouldered past Screamer who was standing at the other end of the corridor laughing about something with a few guys from the footy team.

'Speck!' yelled Tiger Girl after him.

But there was no stopping Specky. He was already outside, sprinting home.

3. under pressure

'Mum!' shouted Specky, bursting through the front door.

'Simon?' called Mrs Magee from the kitchen. 'What are you doing home?'

Specky rushed into the kitchen, panting heavily. He had made it home faster than he ever had before.

'What's wrong?' she asked, lowering her cup of coffee onto the counter. 'Are you hurt?'

'Sammy's dead?'

'What are you talking about? Sammy's in the backyard – he's . . .'

Specky didn't wait for his mum to finish her sentence. He had already bolted out the back door. His mother was right. Sammy was alive and well, chewing on a bone.

'Here, Sam! Here, boy!'

Specky hugged the black cocker spaniel tightly – letting him lick his face all over.

'What's going on?' asked Mrs Magee, a few steps behind.

A beeping sound came from Specky's pocket. It was a text message on his mobile. It read:

> *It's a trick! Screamer made that kid tell u a lie.*
> *Your dog is not dead. TG*

Specky shook his head. He dropped his face into the palms of his hands.

'Simon? Tell me what's going on,' his mum said, quietly.

'Nothing,' he sighed, standing up to go back inside.

'It doesn't look like nothing,' Mrs Magee said.

She stood directly in front of Specky and held onto his shoulders.

'Now,' she continued. 'What's going on?'

'Nothing,' Specky repeated.

'Simon, you may be a teenager, and you may

think it's uncool to talk to your mother, but I don't want you to brush me off. Understood? It's clear that you're upset. Now what's going on?'

Specky looked the other way and tried to shrug his mum off. But she wasn't letting go, and his arm bumped up against her pregnant belly. She took his chin and made him look directly at her.

'It's all right. I know it's been an awful few days for you,' she said, her voice softening again. 'You'll get through it. It's all going to be okay.'

What came next took Specky by surprise. His bottom lip began to quiver and in the depths of his gut everything he had been through that week – the loss of his scholarship, the adjustment to being back at Booyong, the silent treatment from his mates, even the newspaper article – finally caught up with him and shot to the surface like lava in a volcano.

Specky's eyes welled with tears and before he knew it he was sobbing uncontrollably.

You loser, you're fourteen years old – what the hell are you doing? he thought. You're tougher than this. But he couldn't stop. And for the next couple of minutes he wept in his mother's arms.

'I'm sorry, Mum,' he said, embarrassed. 'I didn't mean to lose it.' Specky sniffed, trying to regain some composure. 'It's just that when I got back I couldn't believe Danny and Robbo were no longer my mates, and now they've totally zoned me out, and the guys on the team don't want me on the side. I figure there's no way I'm gonna play footy where I'm not wanted, but what am I gonna do if I don't play?'

'Shhh . . .' soothed his mother. 'It's all right, darling, you don't need to apologise. Goodness me, I get so frustrated with this whole macho football mentality – as if it's somehow a sign of weakness to show your emotions. What about that lovely young man . . . um, the blond one who plays for . . . now what team is it? Anyway, Rick Newhart, or Reeholt or something like that.'

'Nick Riewoldt, Mum. And he plays for St Kilda,' said Specky, cracking a hint of a smile.

'That's right, Nick Riewoldt. Well, he certainly wasn't afraid to show his emotions when those bullies hurt his shoulder. When they showed him on the telly, tears flowing down his cheeks, I wanted to give him a big hug and tell him everything was going to be all right. Just like now.'

Specky recalled that controversial game when the St Kilda superstar had been badly hurt. Even with the pain of an injured shoulder, he played on. A couple of Brisbane Lions players deliberately targeted his weak shoulder, and the bumps they gave him were the talking point in football circles for weeks to come. Riewoldt did end up off the field and in tears – not due to the pain or the actions of the Lions players, but due to the frustrating possibility that he might miss a lot of the football season, especially since he was captain. It just got the better of him. Riewoldt was one of Specky's heroes and he certainly had not thought anything less of him after that night. It did ease the embarrassment of having broken down in front of his mum. Footballers are no different to anyone else, and emotion is a big part of everyday life. There was no shame in having shed a few tears.

Once his tears had dried, Mrs Magee suggested that maybe he should just stay home from school for the afternoon. It was the end of the week anyway.

'And, Simon, one more thing,' she said. 'Friendship – true lasting friendship – is always tested one way or another. Once things settle down I'm sure Danny and Robbo will come round and see that you still think the world of them both. So don't let their behaviour influence the one thing you're truly passionate about – the thing that makes you happy.'

Beep Beep

It was another text message from Tiger Girl.

> *Get my message? It was a trick.*
> *U coming back?*

Specky texted Tiger Girl. He asked her to tell Johnny what had happened and that he was staying home.

For the rest of the afternoon, Specky bummed around the house, watching TV, playing his PlayStation, and even attempting to do some homework.

CHRISkicks: HEY! What r u doing home?

Specky was online and in front of his computer when the Instant Message box popped up. It was from his girlfriend, Christina. Specky wrote right back.

FOOTYHEAD: Um, long story. Will tell u 2morrow. What r u doing home?

CHRISkicks: Curriculum day – no school. I told u that yesterday. Can't wait 2 see u!

Christina had invited Specky to go to the movies with her and her friends on Saturday night.

CHRISkicks: Is Johnny still coming with u?

FOOTYHEAD: No, he can't make it.

CHRISkicks: What about Danny and Robbo? R u all mates again and r u going 2 play footy 2morrow?

Specky wished it were that simple.

FOOTYHEAD: No.

CHRISkicks: That's so weird. I thought they would all get over it and let u play. Even Screamer.

FOOTYHEAD: Why'd u think that?

CHRISkicks: Just thought they would, that's all. So, what r u gonna do?

FOOTYHEAD: About what?

CHRISkicks: About playing footy!!!!

Specky felt a wave of pressure wash over him.

CHRISkicks: Speck?

Specky's fingers hovered over the keyboard. What should he type?

Maybe Johnny's right, he thought. Maybe I should just rock up tomorrow morning and play, and not worry about what the others think.

CHRISkicks: I gotta go. Cya 2morrow in front of the cinemas, at 6.30pm. xxx
FOOTYHEAD: Cya then!

Later that evening, Specky welcomed his family's banter around the dinner table. It was a good distraction from all his current worries. As usual, Alice was holding court.

'So, I said to Rachel that she should ask David to partner her for the deb 'cause he's always had the hots for her, but she said he has two left feet and can't really dance and she'd rather look good on the dance floor.'

Specky grinned as he watched his parents try to keep up with Alice. She spoke at a million miles an hour, hardly ever taking a breath.

'Anyway, I said I'm so lucky to have a boyfriend like Dieter,' she continued. ''Cause he didn't even blink when I asked him this afternoon to be my partner. We're going to be the best-looking couple out there. And we'll be the best dancers, too. It's a good thing Dieter is used to performing in front of crowds. I know I'm gonna be so nervous on the night, but he'll keep me calm, that's for sure!'

'Yeah, right. I don't think so,' laughed Specky.

'What? What did you say?' snapped Alice.

'Nothing.'

'Yes, you did. You said, *yeah, right. I don't think so*. What's that meant to mean?'

Specky smirked. 'Don't get your knickers in a knot.'

'Simon . . .' warned Mrs Magee.

'Me? Get my knickers in a knot? Um, hello, I'm not the one who was expelled,' said Alice, raising her voice.

'There's no need to bring that up, Alice. You can apologise to your brother right now,' said Mr Magee sharply.

'Why's it always me who has to apologise to

him? Simon always stirs and baits me! He gets away with everything.'

Alice pouted and turned back to Specky.

'Now, tell me why you said that.'

'I don't have to tell you anything.' Specky opened his mouth and showed off a gob full of mashed potatoes.

'You're really pushing it, you know that? You might think you're smarter than me, but you're not.'

'Ah, but I am,' smirked Specky, infuriating his sister even more. 'You have to get up early to catch me out.'

The doorbell sounded.

'Alice, that's enough!' ordered Mr Magee, as he got up from his chair. 'Both of you, stop acting like babies. We'll have one in the house before long, and you lot need to grow up. You're teenagers, for goodness sake! Start acting like it!'

Mr Magee left the dining room to answer the door, while Specky and Alice silently glared at each other in between bites. A few moments later, Mr Magee returned to the kitchen with an unexpected visitor.

'Coach Pate!' Specky nearly choked on his dinner.

'Sorry for disturbing you all at tea time,' she said.

'No, not at all. Please sit down. Have you eaten?' Mrs Magee asked, standing up.

'Thank you, Jane, I'm fine. I promise I won't take up much of your time. I just dropped by because I wanted to talk to you and to Simon about footy tomorrow.'

Specky suddenly lost his appetite. Alice gave him one last evil look then excused herself and went upstairs.

'I understand it's been a big week for you all, and I would understand if you said no, Simon, but I really would like you to play tomorrow, despite the pressure you're getting from your teammates not to. I do have a good reason for asking.'

'We'd like him to play, too,' said Mrs Magee.

Mr Magee nodded his agreement.

Coach Pate continued.

'Simon is one of the most talented footballers I have ever coached and . . .'

Specky squirmed in his chair.

'. . . it would be a terrible shame to lose him

as a player. We still have his number-five jumper for him.

'It's important for you all to know that the squad for the Victorian Under Fifteen Schoolboys team is being picked at the moment, and that one of the selectors has informed us that he'll be at the game tomorrow. I think it's pretty clear that Simon has a great chance of making that squad and could end up making the actual side.'

The Victorian Under 15 Schoolboys team plays every year in the National Carnival against all the other States and Territories. It is one of the most sought-after and prestigious honours a schoolboy footballer can hope to achieve. Specky knew that some of the greatest players ever to play Aussie Rules football had come through the Victorian Schoolboys team and he had often wondered what it would be like to play on the team. He had never really allowed himself to believe that he might be good enough to make it, though. It was incredible to hear that Coach Pate thought he could be chosen for the squad, at least. But that was just the beginning. Once the squad was announced, several training sessions took place, and the number of players was reduced as the weeks went by. A final trial match would then be played to find out which players would form the actual team. That game, if Specky was fortunate enough to make it, would be the biggest test of his career so far. It would be against the very best schoolboy footballers in the whole of Victoria, and he got nervous just thinking about it.

'Well, we can't deny the fact that football has lately caused a lot of disruptions in your schooling, Simon,' said Mrs Magee, as if she were a lawyer giving her final arguments to the jury. 'But I think it would be good for you to get back into a routine, and that would, of course, include doing what you love most. It sounds like a very exciting opportunity, too. Ultimately the decision is up to you, though. We will never pressure you into doing something that you don't want to do.'

Specky's stomach churned as his dad and Coach Pate turned to hear his response. Whatever his mum said, the pressure was on. What was he going to do? Could he really face his teammates and still play?

'Well? Don't keep Coach Pate waiting,' urged Mr Magee. 'Are you going to play tomorrow or not?'

Specky took a deep breath.

'Yeah,' he gulped. 'Yeah, I am.'

4. kick it to me

Specky couldn't remember the last time he had had a gut full of butterflies like this before a match. Coach Pate had specifically told him to warm up at home and arrive only fifteen minutes before the game. Specky hadn't asked her why. He had guessed that she probably wanted to have a last-minute talk to the team about the fact that he was coming in to play.

As he approached the change rooms, he could see his teammates and their parents already making their way out on to Booyong High's oval.

'Hey, Specky, man!'

Specky was happy that Johnny was one of the first to greet him.

'Hey! Back in action again?' he said.

'Yep. Y'know, I've been hanging out for this day. I reckon me collarbone is stronger than before,' smiled Johnny. 'So, we just had a team meeting.'

'I thought so,' said Specky. 'And?'

'It's all good. Everyone accepts that you're back in the team. They're all cool about it.'

'Really?'

Specky wasn't so sure. He caught his mum and dad smiling at him as they joined Johnny's dad and the other parents on the boundary line.

'Hey!'

'Hi!'

'G'day, Speck!'

Some of Specky's teammates, including the Bombay Bullet, Gobba and Einstein said hello as they jogged past.

Maybe everything *is* cool, thought Specky.

The last boys to come out of the rooms were Danny, Robbo and Screamer – their stares fixed on Specky.

Specky nodded and grunted an uncomfortable, 'G'day!'

Screamer sped up a little and brushed past,

trying to nudge his elbow into Specky – but Specky sidestepped and managed to get out of the way.

'Welcome back, loser,' grumbled Screamer over his shoulder.

Specky ignored him as he watched Danny and Robbo approach.

'Hiya,' he croaked.

Specky's old mates responded with a cold shrug and jogged away after the rest of the team.

So much for everyone being cool about me being back, Specky thought. This is gonna be interesting.

Coach Pate had put Specky at centre half-forward and Screamer at full-forward. The Booyong High Lions were playing their longtime rivals the Beacon Hill Falcons, and were looking to maintain their two-game winning streak.

As much as Specky was excited about the prospect of playing football again, he couldn't ignore the fact that he was feeling uneasy. The best part about being involved in a sport like football was feeling that you were part of a team, and right now Specky definitely felt like an outsider.

Maybe it's just me, he thought. Maybe I'm over-reacting. When the game starts, it'll be okay . . . I hope.

Specky ran to his position and waited for the bounce of the ball.

The game was competitive and tight right from the start, as it always was against the Falcons. Specky was working harder than ever to try and impress his teammates and let them know that he was determined to make a contribution and help them to victory. But, as hard as he tried, he just couldn't seem to get his hands on the football.

Suddenly, Specky saw Danny break free from the pack at half-back and stream forward, taking a bounce as he looked up the field, searching for a target.

It was a familiar scene for Specky – it had played itself out on the football field since he and Danny were ten years old.

A smile crept over Specky's face as he watched the little Italian dynamo run with the ball. Specky waited patiently before making his lead.

He knew Danny's game so well that he could anticipate, perfectly, when he would look to pass the ball.

At exactly the right moment, Specky doubled back behind his opponent and made a perfect lead into the open spaces of the forward line. There was no one within twenty metres of him.

'DANNY!'

Danny looked at Specky and for a split second it appeared as though he was going to pass the ball right onto his chest.

Then, at the final moment, Danny ignored Specky and decided to have another bounce. The Falcons rover who had been chasing Danny couldn't believe his luck, and with an extra effort, lunged at him and tackled him to the ground.

The Booyong crowd groaned as the Falcons player was awarded a free kick, and the ball rebounded to the other end of the ground for a Falcons goal.

Specky stood there with his hands on his hips, not believing what had just happened.

'Mate, I was in the clear!' he yelled to Danny. 'Why didn't you pass it to me?'

Danny guiltily looked the other way.

'Don't worry about it, Castellino,' Screamer butted in. 'Magee will just have to realise that he can't walk out on this team and come back expecting us to give him an armchair ride. Get your own kicks, superstar!'

And that was the pattern for the rest of the quarter.

No matter how well Specky led, or how good a position he was in, his teammates ignored him – all except for Johnny, who was playing a blinder.

When the half-time siren sounded, Specky found himself walking into the change rooms a dispirited figure. Normally he would be one of the first to jog in, encouraging his fellow players as he went, but right there and then he felt like a total loner.

'Right, sit down quickly!' Coach Pate snapped as she entered the rooms. 'I don't know what's going on out there, but I have never seen you boys play such selfish football. Danny, what were you thinking? You know we always pass the ball to a player in a better position and if you couldn't see Simon out there on his own, then you must have had your eyes closed.'

Specky caught Danny lowering his head, trying desperately to avoid eye contact with him or the coach.

Coach Pate was as mad as anyone had seen her. She never normally shouted, but even when the team ran out onto the ground for the second half, their ears were still ringing.

Specky remembered that at least one State selector was watching this game so he prepared himself for a big half of football.

The ball was knocked out of the centre and he was the first player to get there as he charged in off the square. Specky gathered the ball just as Danny came running past.

Normally Specky would have given the ball off instinctively to Danny, but this time he decided to try and do it all on his own.

Specky faked the handball to Danny and swung around onto his right boot, only to be confronted by the Falcons ruckman. He baulked around him, then dodged and blind-turned another two players – all the while electing not to pass the ball to his teammates in much better positions.

Specky broke clear of the pack and, from fifty metres out, went for goal with a torpedo punt.

To his horror, he watched the ball fly off the side of his boot and sail out on the full – landing on the windscreen of a shiny, new Mercedes Benz, cracking the windscreen in the process.

'Good on ya, hero!' Screamer shouted, so everyone could hear. 'Are you playing for us or just trying to get noticed by the State selectors?'

Specky wanted the ground to swallow him up. He realised immediately that there was some truth in what Screamer had said. He was disappointed in himself and struggled to get another possession for the rest of the quarter.

Coach Pate decided to start Specky on the interchange bench for the last quarter. It was the first time he could remember being dragged during a game for playing poorly.

To add insult to injury, Screamer took over the game and single-handedly put the Lions back in front. It seemed as though Specky might have to sit out the rest of the game, but with only a couple of minutes to go, Coach Pate put him back on, into the forward pocket alongside his rival.

The game was in the balance, with the Lions leading by three points, when Robbo booted the ball forward. Specky set his eyes on the ball and was determined to at last do something right for the day.

As he launched himself into the air, a big knee thumped him in the back of his head.

Specky fell face first into the ground.

When he turned to find out who had used him as a launching pad, he couldn't believe what he saw. There stood Screamer with the footy firmly in his hands.

The crowd roared at the top of their lungs.

'Geez, I don't think I've ever seen someone get up as high as that in my whole life! That was awesome!' Specky heard the Falcons full-back say to his teammate.

'Yeah, I know what you mean. That's the best mark I've ever laid eyes on,' came the reply.

Screamer went back and coolly slotted the footy through the goal as the siren sounded to end the game. Specky's teammates rushed past him to Screamer's side, mobbing him in jubilation. Even the Falcons players seemed keen to shake the hand of the player who had just taken the mark of the year.

As the crowd broke up and the players headed for the change rooms, Specky cut a lonely figure at the back of the pack.

'Well, brother,' said Johnny, waiting to walk off with Specky. 'Of all the car windows you could've smashed, you picked the one that belongs to the Coach of the Victorian Schoolboys.'

Specky's faced dropped. He looked back at the Mercedes to see, standing in front of the car, two men in navy polo shirts with a Big V embroidered on the sleeves. They were chatting to Screamer's father.

Specky recognised one of the men as Jay 'Grub' Gordan.

Grub was renowned as the most successful under-age coach in Australia. His knowledge of football and his ability to recognise and develop young football talent was legendary, and his opinion and assessment of junior players had an enormous influence on those charged with the responsibility of recruiting players to the AFL.

He also had a reputation for being a tough taskmaster who demanded a lot from his players. Football people often referred to him as a 'colourful' character and he carried the nickname 'Grub' from his days playing cricket as an elite wicketkeeper in Victorian and national teams.

Specky had once read that Grub could be very confronting and for young players, who were used to being the best in their teams and had rarely been criticised, his honest and blunt assessment of their performances often took some getting used to. He would not stand for any nonsense and let players know very quickly if they were not playing to the team rules or working hard enough at their game. No one prepared young footballers better than 'Grub' Gordan, and there were hundreds of players that went on to have fantastic careers at AFL level who were very quick to point out that he had been the biggest influence on their football lives.

'I gotta hand it to you, Speck,' Johnny chuckled. 'When you stuff up, you stuff up big-time. Don't worry about it. I like BMWs more anyway.'

Specky tried to see the humour in Johnny's comment, but couldn't.

'Hey, Magee!' smirked Screamer, standing in the doorway of the change rooms. 'Think the State selectors have learnt a lot today?'

'Yeah, whatever,' Specky grunted in reply.

'Well, at least I was right when I told your girl-friend we didn't need you back in the team. You should go back to Gosmore. Oh, but that's right, you can't – 'cause you got expelled.'

Specky let the comment slide – he was distracted by Screamer's mention of Christina. 'What are ya talking about? When did you talk to Christina?'

'The other night.'

'What?'

'Yeah, she called me and said I better con-vince your mates to let you back in the team. Not likely!' Screamer laughed, and Johnny gave him a disgusted look.

Specky desperately didn't want to believe it. Why would Christina talk to Screamer about him? She and Screamer were still friends – although Specky could never figure out what she saw in him. She knew how much they hated each other, though, and he was sure Screamer was lying.

'Yeah, as if,' said Specky.

'Say what ya want,' Screamer sneered. 'But trust you, Magee, to get your girlfriend to fight your battles for ya. Ya wimp!'

Specky had no comeback.

5. questions

'Hey! Gotta talk to you!'

Alice barged into Specky's bedroom.

'What are you doing in the dark?' she asked, switching on the light.

Specky had spent the entire afternoon in his bedroom stewing over the rotten morning he'd had. He just felt like hiding away and listening to AFL matches live on the radio.

'Get out! I'm listening to Rexy,' he snapped at Alice.

'That dude that says Yabbada, Yabbada, Yibiddy or whatever it is? What is it with him, anyway? I can't understand a word he says. He doesn't even know the proper names of the players.'

'That's what I'd expect from you, Alice,' said

Specky. 'That's what makes it so much fun to listen to him. He knows all the players, but he gives them their own special nicknames. If you had any idea about footy you'd know what I mean.'

'I know who's hot and who's not, and that's all that matters. Hello? Remember I met Shane Crawford once.'

Specky shook his head, recalling the day his sister and her best friend, Rachel, had gone gaga while waiting for the Hawthorn champion after training one night to get his autograph.

'Yeah, well, he wouldn't know you if you turned up in his bowl of Weeties. You're such a pain.'

'As if I care! I'm over him now. Give me Ben Cousins or Gary Ablett Jnr or Brodie Holland any day – they're seriously hot! Anyway, I gotta tell you something.'

'No, I wanna hear the post-match comments. Now, get lost!'

But Alice wasn't budging.

'But I think you might wanna hear this.'

'I don't wanna know . . . *Mum! Alice is bugging me!*'

'All right, all right! I'll leave then. Can't interrupt His Royal Highness when the precious footy is on.'

'Yeah, whatever, stuff footy!' Specky mumbled under his breath.

Alice stopped abruptly halfway out the door and whipped around with a shocked look on her face.

'Did you just say "stuff footy"?'

'Yeah,' Specky grunted.

'Are you my brother or an imposter?'

Alice tried to make light of Specky's comment, but he could tell it had really thrown her. He couldn't believe what he had just said himself.

'Are you okay?' she asked, sounding more serious now.

Specky nodded, but wondered if he was. For the first time in his life he had bagged the game he had always been so passionate about, and this scared him a little.

'Don't you like footy anymore?'

Specky's mind was racing a million miles an hour. He was silent for a second, then he shrugged.

'Is footy really for me? Look where it's got me. Expelled. No mates. Is it worth it if I'm not having any fun? Maybe I should play something else.'

'You're not serious, are ya?' Alice kept on at him. 'Or are you?'

Specky turned his back on Alice. 'I don't want to talk about it.'

'Well, if you give up footy, then at least you'll have more time for dancing,' Alice teased.

'I didn't say I was gonna give up footy, I was just saying – hang on, *dancing*? What do you mean, dancing?'

'You'll find out,' smirked Alice. 'Let's just say I know something you don't. And it's got to do with dancing.'

As Alice shot a wicked smile in his direction, the phone rang.

'I'll get it!' she yelled, dashing out of Specky's bedroom, only to return a few moments later.

'It's for you,' she said, handing the phone over to Specky and pulling another goofy expression.

'Hello?'

'Hi, Speck.'

It was Tiger Girl.

'Hi, what's up?' asked Specky.

'Um, Speck, remember I wanted to ask you something yesterday, before that Year Seven kid interrupted us?'

'Oh, yeah. What was it?'

'Um, well . . .' She trailed off.

'What's wrong?' Specky said. Tiger Girl didn't sound like her usual confident self.

'Um, nothing. I was just, um . . .'

Specky looked up to see that Alice was still standing there. He waved at her to get out. She didn't.

'I was just wondering if . . .'

'Yeah?'

Tiger Girl cleared her throat. 'Well, I was wondering if you would be my debutante partner?'

'Debutante partner?' repeated Specky, taken aback.

Alice sniggered and began to mouth, 'She lurves you . . .'

'Rack off!' snapped Specky.

'Oh, okay. I'll ask someone else then,' stuttered Tiger Girl.

'No, not you!' said Specky quickly, back into the phone. 'I wasn't telling *you* to rack off. My sister's bugging me. Hold on!'

Specky pushed Alice out of his room and slammed the door shut. He could still hear her giggling in the corridor.

'Sorry about that,' he said, returning to Tiger Girl.

'So, do you wanna be my partner? You can say no, if you want. It's just that all my old friends from last year are now in Year Ten and they're all doing their deb with the Year Eleven girls and, well, I didn't want to miss out . . .'

Specky had never heard Tiger Girl sound so nervous before.

If only she knew how nervous *I* am, he thought, his mouth drying up. I can't dance for nuts!

Specky had a flash of what he had told the Great McCarthy – about not being a wimp. He had to practise what he preached . . .

'Yeah, sure,' he mumbled, reluctantly.

'Really? You'll be my partner, then?'

'Yeah, I will.'

'Great! Thanks, Speck. This is gonna be so much fun. Our first dance rehearsal is Sunday afternoon at the school hall, and then every Sunday from then on. I'll tell you more about it when I see you at school. Anyway, I gotta go. See ya!'

Specky had no sooner hung up the phone when Alice burst back into the room.

'So, did you say yes?'

Specky nodded.

'I knew she was gonna call you. Rachel told me that she had heard from her sister's best friend's cousin that she was thinking of asking you. Anyway, it's gonna be weird having my little brother in the some debutante group. Just don't hang around me and try to be my friend.'

'Yeah, right,' scoffed Specky, wondering what he had just got himself into.

'So, how will Christina react? She won't get jealous, will she?'

'Christina? Oh hell! Christina!'

Specky jumped off the bed and grabbed his jacket.

'What's going on?' Alice asked, stepping aside.

'What time is it?' Specky panicked. 'I'm meant to be meeting up with her to see a movie round about now – and I forgot all about it!'

'Stop saying sorry. You weren't that late. I'm just glad you're here,' said Christina, sitting between Specky and her friends, Sophie and Emily, in the dark cinema. The movie had just started.

'SHHH!' hissed a man sitting directly behind them.

'Yeah, but it would've been good to be able to talk to you instead of rushing in here at the last minute. I wanted to ask you something,' whispered Specky.

'What?'

'*SHHHH!*'

'Do you wanna go outside, just for a sec?' asked Specky.

'But we'll miss the movie,' said Christina, surprised.

'Okay, yeah, then maybe after.'

'No, let's go now, but just for a couple of minutes. I can tell something's up,' added Christina. She whispered to her friends that they'd be back soon.

Specky and Christina shuffled their way out of the row, trying to ignore all the people shushing and whispering 'get out of the way' and 'move your big head'.

'Look, I really am sorry I was late,' said Specky again, once they were out in the lobby. 'Tiger Girl called me. She asked me to be her partner for her debutante.'

'Cool! I can't wait to do mine next year,' exclaimed Christina. 'That *is* exciting!'

'You don't mind?' said Specky, relieved.

'Mind what?'

'You know, Tiger Girl and me, dancing together?'

'Of course not,' smiled Christina. 'I know you're just good friends. You *are* just good friends, aren't you?'

'Yeah, yeah, we are,' nodded Specky.

'Then great! By the time you're my partner you'll be a specky-tacular dancer.'

Specky and Christina groaned in unison at the bad joke.

'So, is that what you got me out here for? Because you were worried I'd be jealous?' asked Christina. 'That's so sweet!' She gave him a kiss on the cheek.

Specky didn't want to ruin the moment, but he had to ask . . . 'Well, not exactly,' he said. 'Look, um . . . I didn't believe it when Screamer told me today, and I bet he was only making it up to stir me, but I was just wondering . . . Did you talk to him about me earlier this week?'

Christina paused for a second. 'Yeah, I did,' she said.

'You did?' Specky's jaw tightened and his heart jumped a few extra beats.

'Wh . . . why?' he stuttered.

''Cause I thought he was being a jerk and I was gonna say that he should tell the others to let you play or else I'd tell them that he . . .' She trailed off into silence.

'That he what?' asked Specky.

'Nothing. Don't worry about it!' snapped Christina defensively.

But Specky wasn't going to let it drop. 'No, you were about to say, I'd tell them that he . . . what? What have you got on Screamer?' he demanded.

Christina coughed nervously. She was obviously hiding something.

'Is there something about him you know and no one else does? Were you gonna use that against him to arrange it so that I could play?'

'What! Where did that come from?'

'From you!' said Specky. 'Remember last year when you were going out with him and you said to me that he has other interests besides footy. Remember? Has it got to do with that?'

Christina looked surprised. 'You have a

memory like an elephant.' She folded her arms. 'Look, just forget about it. He told me to mind my own business anyway. And now he's not talking to me – he's mad that I even suggested it.'

'So why not tell me what the big secret is then?'

'Because I had second thoughts, and I can't. It's not really like me to do something like that, and I don't want to hurt him. Besides, you ended up playing today – so everything's cool.'

'Yeah, it's perfect,' Specky replied, sarcastically.

'Speck, if you're jealous or something, then you shouldn't be. I was just trying to help you. I don't know what the big deal is, anyway,' Christina added, raising her voice a little. 'You know we chat occasionally.'

'The big deal,' huffed Specky, 'is that I don't need anyone sticking up for me. I can look after myself.'

An awkward pause followed, while Specky and Christina both realised that they were having their first major argument. Their faces were flushed with frustration.

'Then suit yourself . . . but I thought I wasn't just *anyone*. Excuse me for caring!'

Christina turned and raced off back into the cinema.

'Man, I'm an idiot,' Specky sighed.

6. out of the ordinary

'Simon?'

Specky's dad entered the study to find him playing his PlayStation.

'What's up?' Specky asked, not taking his eyes off the screen.

'It's Sunday morning,' Mr Magee said, stating the obvious.

'Yeah, so?'

'Why aren't you watching *Sensational Sunday*?'

Sensational Sunday was a spin-off from *Sensational Stuff*. It was Specky's second favourite TV footy show and, except for the time he spent boarding at Gosmore, he had watched it religiously every Sunday morning. But not *this* Sunday morning.

'Oh, yeah,' mumbled Specky. 'Nah, I don't feel like watching it today.'

Specky glanced back to catch his father pulling the same bemused face Alice had made when he had bagged footy.

After the miserable time he had had yesterday, and that included his night out with Christina, Specky wanted to find out what a day without footy would be like. And that meant not even mentioning it or watching it on TV.

'Are you okay?' asked Mr Magee.

'Yeah, I just wanna do something different this morning,' replied Specky.

'Well, there's nothing wrong with that. Would you like to come with me? I'm off to meet a local artist – his watercolours are absolutely brilliant. I'm hoping to exhibit his work at the gallery.'

'Um, nah, it's okay, Dad. I was actually planning to go for a ride.'

'Well, if you change your mind, I'm leaving in twenty minutes.'

Riding his bike was the most practical way for Specky to get around, but he also knew that plenty of players used bike riding as a way of cross-training for the football season. It maintained their aerobic fitness without putting the stress and strain on their legs that miles and miles of repetitive running was inclined to do. He could actually tell that it improved his fitness and enabled him to run harder in a game of football.

Specky didn't change his mind, and within a few minutes he was riding his bike around the streets of Camberwell.

He headed towards the shops, but then took a detour into Robbo's street. Specky wasn't exactly sure why he had done that, but he continued to peddle towards his old friend's house anyway. As he rolled by the Roberts' place, he contemplated stopping and knocking on the front door.

He's probably watching *Sensational Sunday*, he thought. Maybe he'll ask me what I'm doing here, and I'll say I've just come to hang out, and then he'll say that's cool and . . .

'Josh, where's the bucket?'

It was Robbo's dad shouting from the side of the house. He was making his way toward the road. Specky suddenly felt nervous and quickly crunched down on his pedals and took off down the street.

A few blocks later, Specky was almost at Danny's house. As he cruised by the Booyong rover's home, Danny's uncle Joe suddenly hopped out of his car – directly in front of him. Specky slammed on his brakes, and just avoided running straight into him.

'Whoah,' gasped Uncle Joe, falling back against the side of the car.

'Sorry,' said Specky.

'That's all right,' he said. 'I should've looked before I opened the door. Simon, isn't it? Danny's mate?'

Specky nodded. He had met Danny's uncle and most of his family several times before. They were a huge Italian family that always hung out together. Specky had gone to the footy with them on a few occasions – they were all diehard Collingwood supporters. In fact, Uncle Joe was wearing a Collingwood jacket and cap.

'So, you coming to the G with us today, Simon?' he asked. 'See the mighty Pies?'

'No,' said Specky sadly.

'Oh well, maybe next time. It's gonna be a big game. I know Danny's looking forward to it. We all are. It'll be a good distraction. My mum,

Danny's grandmother, has been ill lately, so it'll be good for us to get a bit of air and have a break from it all.'

Even though Specky was trying to have a footy-free day, he suddenly remembered why football meant so much to him and to hundreds of thousands of other people. For many it was one of the highlights of their lives. For lots of people work was something that they had to do to put food on the table and pay the bills. It was not necessarily something that they got passionate about. But footy . . . that was a whole different matter.

It didn't matter what else was going on in their day-to-day existence – family problems, work or school hassles or just a bit of a rough patch – they could rely on their football side to give them something to look forward to. It could be a tremendous bonding exercise, a social time that united family and friends. For a couple of hours every weekend, nothing else mattered other than screaming their lungs out for the footy side they loved and barracked for.

Specky was always amazed at how devoted supporters were to their team. He could just imagine footy-obsessed families like Danny's trying to plan a wedding. The groom would say:

'Sorry, darl, we can't get married in February – that's when the pre-season competition starts. March to the end of August is out of the question – can't afford to miss one of the home and away games. And as for the month of September, well forget it – finals time, baby! And October is a little difficult, because Australia take on Ireland in the International Rules and, well, you know, you've got to be patriotic and all. The boys will be back into pre-season in November and you know I like to see how the new recruits are progressing. I tell you what, they break up for Christmas around the twentieth of December and don't start again until the fourth or fifth of January. Maybe we can book a church at that time . . . Forget about a honeymoon, though. I can't miss that first training session after Christmas.'

Specky knew that Danny's grandmother was as big a fan of Collingwood as Danny was. 'I'm sorry. I hope she gets better,' he said.

'Thanks, mate. Look, let me get Danny for you.'

'Nah, that's okay,' said Specky quickly. 'I'm just on my –'

'Danny!' Uncle Joe suddenly shouted at the top of his lungs.

Before Specky knew it, he was tearing down the street away from Danny's uncle as if he were a Tour de France sprint champion.

'Man, that was close,' he puffed under his breath once he had turned the corner.

Specky continued to ride his bike for the next hour or so. He rode aimlessly, eventually ending up in a suburb he didn't know that well. When he stopped to rest and buy himself a drink, Specky noticed a large crowd of teenagers snaking their way into a bookstore. He rolled his bike toward them to have a closer look.

'What's going on?' Specky asked a boy about his own age, waiting at the end of the line.

'It's a book signing,' said the boy, as if Specky should've known. 'The latest *Hanger MacPherson* book is out today.'

Specky had heard of the popular series of books about an up-and-coming footy champion named Hanger MacPherson, written by AFL legend Barry Line and author Fernando Serena. He had read the first two books in the series himself a couple of years ago and really enjoyed them.

'I can't wait to read this next one,' added the boy excitedly. 'They're the best books ever.'

Specky thought of his Gosmore Grammar friend Worm and how he'd get a kick out of talking to this guy. He wondered if he should wait in line himself and get a copy – even though he had promised himself he wouldn't do anything connected to footy for the day.

But suddenly he was distracted. 'Screamer?' he choked. Out of the corner of his eye, Specky had spotted a familiar figure hopping off a tram. 'What's he doing here?'

Specky quickly ducked behind a telephone pole. The boy he had been talking to gave him an odd look.

Damn Screamer, Specky thought. What's he up to now?

Specky watched his rival walk away from the bookstore and turn left into a side street. Specky followed as if he were some kind of secret commando spy. He dodged between buildings and in and out of the way of pedestrians – all very difficult to do whilst wheeling his bike. When Specky turned into a short street lined with trees, he caught Screamer heading into a building a few doors down.

Specky slowly approached the building, which looked like a small public library.

What is this place? Specky wondered. He caught a glimpse of Screamer through the window adjacent to the entrance.

Specky ducked to the ground beneath the opened window. The bike landed on him. It hurt. He only just stopped himself from groaning out loud.

Phew, that was close, thought Specky.

He got into a squatting position and listened carefully.

'Mr Johnson, it's two minutes past,' came a man's disapproving voice. 'Please be early next time. Talent does not give you a golden ticket to be late. Now, let's begin with some Schubert.'

A few seconds later, beautiful classical piano music filled the room. Specky screwed up his face, confused. He had to see what was going on. Slowly he edged his way up to the window and took a peek inside.

'No way,' he gasped, under his breath. Specky couldn't believe his eyes.

Screamer was playing the piano.

7. quick step

Shaking his head in complete shock, Specky watched Screamer play the piano as if he were some concert pianist. Standing beside Screamer was a Chinese man looking over his shoulder as he played.

They both had their backs to Specky and were totally focused on the music.

So, I bet this is what Christina meant by having other talents, thought Specky. But why would Screamer want to hide this? He's great! Maybe 'cause it doesn't go with being a tough jerk the rest of the time.

As Specky listened to Screamer's extraordinary playing he was reminded of some AFL players who had displayed talents in other areas. *Sensational Stuff* had run a competition to find out who was the best singer in the AFL and Specky had thought that the high-flying Demon, Russell Robertson, had been pretty cool. He could sing and play the guitar. Specky also remembered that Luke Ball from St Kilda had been a champion cricketer as a schoolboy, former Demon Todd Viney had once played tennis against Boris Becker, and that Richmond star Nathan Brown wrote poetry. He'd also heard that retired Kangaroo Leigh Colbert had his pilot's licence, and even that James Hird, the Essendon champion, had attended ballet classes as a youngster. He knew that just because someone excelled in one area, it didn't mean that they couldn't also be talented in a whole different area of life. In fact, all clubs encouraged their players to develop interests outside of football to keep them fresh and to ensure that they explored everything life had to offer.

When Screamer stopped playing, his teacher nodded approvingly. 'Even better than last week,' he said.

'Mr Li,' said Screamer, sounding a bit nervous. 'Mum said that you had something to tell me?'

'Yes, Derek, I do. But first, come with me.'

Screamer stood up from the piano and walked with his teacher toward the window. Specky ducked just in time. He could hear Screamer and Mr Li draw closer.

If I run for it, they'll see me for sure, thought Specky.

He had no choice but to stay dead still. Screamer and Mr Li stopped about a metre from the window.

'Look out there and tell me what you see,' Mr Li said.

'Trees, um . . . a red Holden Commodore, some buildings, a sparrow . . .'

'No, no, no. Beyond the cars and trees, Derek – look again,' said Mr Li. 'There's a big world out there. And you deserve to see it. Music will take you to see it.' After a pause, he continued. 'Derek, one of the greatest pianists of our time, Yoshio Aihara, has announced that he will be coming to Australia to conduct a series of master classes for young up-and-coming musicians. But he is only taking five students and auditions will be held in a few weeks' time. I believe that out of all my students, you should be the one to try out for this.'

Again, another long pause followed. Specky was holding his breath. He hoped they wouldn't come any closer to the window and discover him there. He looked around to see a woman walking her dog giving him a suspicious look. Fortunately, she kept moving.

'Well, the look on your face says it all,' said Mr Li.

Specky wished he could see the expression on Screamer's face. He thought again how surreal this whole situation was.

'Are you still practising at your mother's work after school each day?'

'Yeah, except when I've got footy training,' replied Screamer. 'You always ask me that – every week!'

'And I will keep asking you. Practise. Practise. Practise. I can't say it enough.'

Mr Li and Screamer moved away from the window and moments later Screamer was playing the piano again.

'Hey, you!' A man walking toward the building called out to Specky. Specky didn't respond, he just struggled to get his bike upright – his legs had gone to sleep. Then he heard Mr Li say,

'I wonder what's going on out there?'

Specky was busted. He had to get out of there before Screamer spotted him. He wheeled his bike as fast as he could toward the street, and took a running jump onto it. Once again he found himself crunching down on his pedals like a mad man – until he was out of sight.

Riding home, Specky wondered if Screamer had seen him – and what, if anything, he could do with this newfound information about his long-time rival.

Later that afternoon, Specky found himself standing to attention beside Tiger Girl, the Great McCarthy, Alice, and about twenty-five other debutante couples at their first rehearsal in the Booyong High School Hall. The dance teachers, who were also the organisers of the event, were an elderly husband-and-wife team – Mr and Mrs Twiddle. Their seventy-five-year-old neighbour, Shirley, was the pianist.

'Quiet now, please!' said Mrs Twiddle, stepping forward.

Specky glanced across to catch the Great McCarthy acting peculiar. He was bowing his head, grunting, '*C'mon, c'mon,*' under his breath. Alice nudged him in the ribs to pay attention.

Specky turned to Tiger Girl, and she smiled. He grinned back, hiding the nerves he felt about being the youngest there.

'Right, girls, or should I say, young ladies – beautiful, elegant young ladies. Your debutante is an event you will cherish for the rest of your lives,' announced Mrs Twiddle, who sounded remarkably similar to the Queen of England.

'Yes!' yelped the Great McCarthy.

Everyone turned to Dieter. He quickly apologised, saying it was a sneeze. Alice screwed up her face, not looking too pleased with him. On closer inspection, Specky could see a wire running up the back of Dieter's neck and into his ear. Specky realised immediately what was going on – the Great McCarthy was listening to the footy on a radio hidden in his pocket.

'This is the moment when you'll be presented to society not as girls, but as ladies,' continued Mrs Twiddle. 'And while this tradition may be fading in today's modern world, for Nigel and myself it's a ritual that we want to keep alive for many more years to come.'

'Oh, no way!' Dieter blurted out.

Again everyone turned to the Great McCarthy – and again he apologised.

Specky sniggered, finding it hard not to completely crack up. Mrs Twiddle shot a stern look at Dieter, while Alice looked away, embarrassed by her boyfriend.

'Right, where was I?' sniffed Mrs Twiddle.

She went on to discuss what was required over the coming weeks, including the types of dances everyone was to learn.

'In time you'll all be dancing the Pride of Erin, the Boston Two Step, and the Progressive Barn Dance,' Mrs Twiddle said proudly. 'But for now, Nigel and I are going to show you the Swing Waltz. Shirley, music please.'

Specky and the others watched as Mr and Mrs Twiddle swayed and moved as one, as if they were gliding on air. At first everyone, including Specky, laughed and giggled, but the more they watched the more they were impressed. When the Twiddles stopped, everyone cheered and applauded.

'Shirley, you can stop now,' ordered Mrs Twiddle. 'Shirley!'

Shirley was still playing the piano. She was a little hard of hearing. Mr Twiddle eventually had to go and tap her on the shoulder.

'Right, who here among you strapping young men would like to try this with me?' asked Mrs Twiddle.

'YES!' shouted the Great McCarthy.

Specky snorted with laughter. He knew that Dieter was only reacting to the footy commentary in his earpiece – Richmond must've kicked a goal. But now he had dobbed himself in. Mrs Twiddle pushed her way through the group, grabbed Dieter's hand, and dragged him out to the front. Dieter had no idea what was going on.

Everyone laughed nervously for the Great McCarthy – most of all Alice.

'Right, put this hand on my hip and this hand on my hand. Okay, Shirley, music please! SHIRLEY, MUSIC!'

Again everyone burst into fits of laughter as the Great McCarthy shuffled his way through the routine – bumping into Mrs Twiddle and stepping on her feet. After the dance, which had looked more like a wrestling match, Dieter rejoined the rest of them, deeply embarrassed.

'Nice one!' Specky stirred.

'Yeah, well at least the Tigers won. I picked eight this weekend,' Dieter retorted. 'And I wouldn't start hanging it on me if I were you!'

The Great McCarthy shot his hand up.

'Um, Mrs Twiddle . . .'

'What are you doing?' panicked Specky.

'Mrs Twiddle, Simon Magee wishes you had picked him. He's dying to give it a go.'

'What? No, um . . .' stuttered Specky.

But it was too late. Everyone cheered, and before Specky knew it he was hand in hand with Mrs Twiddle.

'Shirley!' yelled Mrs Twiddle, as Specky caught sight of Tiger Girl giving him the thumbs up.

When the music started, Specky stumbled as much as Dieter had, but after a few attempts he got the hang of it.

'That's it. One, two, three . . .' instructed Mrs Twiddle

Specky focused on each step he took as if he were learning a new footy skill, all the while trying to block out the heavy waves of perfume coming at him from Mrs Twiddle.

'Give him a big round of applause, everyone! He's a real natural at this.'

Everyone cheered. Dieter shook his head as if to say 'you lucky bugger, Magee', while Tiger Girl nodded proudly.

Moments later, every couple was attempting the Swing Waltz and by the end of the afternoon most of the students were actually enjoying it.

When Specky returned home he was in such a chipper mood he almost forgot about seeing Screamer that morning and the previous night's argument with Christina. That is until his mother said, 'Do you think Christina will want to join us at the debutante ball?'

Specky sighed. He knew an apology was in order and went to find the phone.

'Hello, Mr Perry. It's Simon here. Can I talk to Christina, please?'

'Sure, Simon, hold on . . .'

Specky wondered how he was going to say he was sorry and if he should bring Screamer up.

'Um, Simon?' Mr Perry had returned to the phone.

'Yes.'

'I'm sorry, but Christina is busy doing a school project and she can't come to the phone at the moment.'

'Oh,' coughed Specky, embarrassed.

Specky could hear Christina whispering to her dad in the background. It was obvious she didn't want to talk to him.

Specky thanked Mr Perry and hung up the phone, dejected. For a second or so he stood in the hallway staring into space. Were Christina and he no longer a couple?

'And then he had to listen to the footy and he wasn't paying any attention to Mrs Twiddle . . .'

Alice was retelling the story to Mrs Magee as they made their way from the lounge room to the kitchen. Mr Magee followed a few steps behind.

'Simon, have you put out the bins? It's bin night,' he said.

Specky nodded and went outside. As he rolled the large green bin out to the front of the house, he thought he heard a rustling sound nearby. He looked around. It was difficult to see much in the dark and a winter fog had set in for the night.

Hmm. Probably just a possum, thought Specky. He shrugged and continued to wheel the bin into position on the nature strip.

Suddenly, a shadow came charging out of the darkness toward Specky. In an instant, he was hit from the side and flung to the ground, as if he had been tackled by Glenn Archer. But it wasn't the Kangaroo star, it was Screamer.

8. say what?

'What the hell were you doing spying on me today, Magee?' Screamer shouted angrily, pinning Specky to the ground.

'Get off me, you psycho!' Specky shouted back, trying to push him away.

For the next few minutes the two boys wrestled each other on the front lawn until Specky's father ran outside to see what all the commotion was about.

'What the hell do you think you're doing?' growled Mr Magee, pulling Screamer off his son.

Screamer batted Mr Magee's hand away – and sprinted off down the street.

'What's going on?' snapped Specky's dad, turning to face him.

'Nothing, he's just psychotic,' puffed Specky, catching his breath and brushing the grass off his shirt.

'Simon! No one attacks you out of the blue like that for no reason. Now tell me why you two were fighting,' ordered Mr Magee.

Specky told his dad about how he had discovered something about Screamer that most people didn't know. He didn't want to get into specifics.

'And that gives him a reason to attack you?' Specky had never seen his father so angry.

'Dad, he didn't *attack* me. You make him sound like he's some mugger or something. Look, it's cool. Let's just leave it.'

Judging from the expression on Mr Magee's face, Specky could tell it definitely wasn't cool with him.

'Wait by the car, I'm going inside to get my keys,' he said angrily, storming back into the house.

'Your keys? What for? Dad, wait! No, can't we just . . .'

There was nothing Specky could say. He knew he wouldn't be able to stop his dad from going to speak to Screamer's parents.

This is gonna be ugly, Specky thought, as he and his father pulled up in front of the Johnson house.

'Yes?' asked Screamer's mother, answering the door. She hadn't recognised Specky or his dad.

'Mrs Johnson, I'm David Magee. Your son goes to school with my son, Simon.'

'Oh, yes, the Magees. How can I help you?'

'Derek just attacked Simon on the front lawn of my house and I –'

'Who's at the door?' came a booming voice from down the hall.

It was Mr Johnson.

'Magees! What are you doin' here?' he snarled, pushing Screamer's mum aside and stepping toward the doorway.

That poor woman, Specky thought, being married to Mr Johnson.

Specky's dad repeated what he had said to Mrs Johnson.

'Well, your son probably deserved it,' scoffed Mr Johnson.

'Excuse me!' retorted Mr Magee. 'It was unprovoked. Maybe this should be taken up with the police.'

'Go ahead, Magee! Call them! See if I care. But your son hasn't been the golden child himself recently, has he? Being expelled only a week ago and now back to cause trouble.'

Specky winced. He wished he were anywhere else except in the middle of this awkward confrontation.

'But just to prove you wrong, Magee,' continued Mr Johnson. 'Let's hear from Derek. Derek! Come 'ere!'

Screamer made his way into the hallway, brushed past his mum, and shuffled up beside his dad. He shot Specky a dirty look and then darted his eyes downward.

'Did you attack Magee?' asked Mr Johnson.

'His name is Simon,' said Specky's dad.

Screamer looked toward his mum, who was visibly upset.

'Yeah,' he grunted, to Specky's surprise. He had thought Screamer would deny it.

'Why would you do that?' asked Mrs Johnson. 'Did he do something to you? Were you defending yourself?'

Mr Magee jumped in and told them everything Specky had said to him – that Specky had discovered something about Screamer and that he had attacked him because he didn't want Specky revealing his secret.

'And what's the secret? What's the big mystery then?' sneered Mr Johnson.

Specky saw Screamer's face go pale and noticed that his mother, who was standing behind Mr Johnson, suddenly looked very alarmed.

'Simon didn't tell me,' answered Mr Magee, giving Specky an annoyed look.

'What's he talking about?' exclaimed Screamer's dad, turning to his son. 'What does Magee know about you that I don't?'

It suddenly dawned on Specky that Screamer's dad didn't know anything about his son's talent for playing the piano. He looked past Screamer and Mr Johnson and saw Mrs Johnson looking at him and silently shaking her head.

'It's nothing!' Specky blurted out.

'What?' said Mr Johnson and Mr Magee together.

'It was all a game! It's a game that some of the boys at school have been playing all week – to see how many ambushes we can do on each other,' lied Specky. 'I got Screamer, I mean Derek, the other day, and he was just getting me back, isn't that right?'

Specky couldn't believe what he was saying – and neither could Screamer.

What followed next was an embarrassing few minutes for Mr Magee and Specky as they apologised to the Johnsons. On the drive home, Mr Magee was so upset with Specky he was speechless.

'Dad,' Specky said softly as they drove into their street. 'I was just protecting Screamer back there. I made that story up.'

Mr Magee slammed on the brakes. Specky explained everything to his dad.

'Well, I wish you had told me all of this earlier,' sighed Mr Magee, looking somewhat relieved and less angry than he had a few minutes ago.

'But why? Why protect a kid who has given you so much trouble?'

Specky wondered about that, too.

The following morning at school, Specky decided not to tell Tiger Girl or Johnny about his eventful weekend. He wanted time to work out what he could do to fix his relationship with Christina, and what, if anything, he would say to Screamer the next time he saw him. Which was sooner than Specky expected.

Before his first class, while Specky was getting his books out of his locker, he felt a small shove in his back. It was Screamer.

'Thanks,' he mumbled. 'For not saying anything last night.'

Specky was shocked. It was the first time Screamer had spoken to him politely.

'Yeah, well, whatever. It's okay,' replied Specky. 'But why doesn't your old man know?'

''Cause he doesn't need to know, all right?' snapped Screamer, back to his normal gruff self. 'And you better not tell anyone, Magee, or I swear I'll –'

'Yeah, relax will ya!' said Specky. 'I'm not gonna say anything . . .' he paused. 'I'm not gonna say anything *if* . . .'

'If what?'

'If you tell the boys in the team the truth – that I was never up myself and never once thought I was better than them. All I want is for them to treat me like any other member of the team. I don't expect any favours. I just want to play and train hard and earn my spot back and help us win as many games as we can.'

Screamer nodded – for a moment, he seemed like a regular guy.

'All right, you're on,' he said. 'But for your information, I might've planted the seed of the idea not to take you back. But it was Danny and Robbo who ended up convincing the others. They're the ones who felt you did the dirty on them. I just pushed that 'cause I hate your guts, Magee, plain and simple!'

Screamer turned to head off to class.

'Hey!' Specky called after him. 'I pretty much hate your guts, too, but I think you're a good player – and I'm not talking about footy. You should audition for that Japanese dude.'

For a split second, Specky could see Screamer was taken aback. But he was definitely back to his old self.

'Get stuffed, Magee!' he answered.

9. baulk and talk

At recess, Specky sent a text message to Christina. It was short and simple:

Sorry – Speck x

Specky waited, but there was no response.

'Specky, man!' yelled Johnny, waving him over to have a kick of a footy with some of the Year 10 boys.

'Speck!' came another familiar voice, this time from behind. It was Robbo.

That was quick, thought Specky as his old mate made his way over to him. Screamer must've said something to him already.

'Hey,' nodded Specky.

'Hey.'

'I know what you're gonna say and you don't have to worry about it,' Specky added quickly. 'It's all good.'

'I know I don't have to worry. But Danny's pretty upset.'

'Sorry?' Specky asked, realising that he and Robbo were talking about two completely different things.

'Yeah, Danny,' said Robbo. 'His grandmother died yesterday. He's gonna be away for the whole week.'

Specky was stunned.

'Oh, um, I knew she had been sick . . . I hope Danny's okay.'

'I called him before school this morning and he couldn't stop balling his eyes out. He's pretty cut up.'

'C'mon, Speck!' yelled Johnny again.

Specky motioned to Johnny that he'd join him in a second.

'So, what did ya mean before when you said you knew what I was gonna say?' asked Robbo.

'Nothing,' shrugged Specky. 'Anyway, I'm gonna have a kick. You wanna join us?'

'Um, nah. Gonna get somethin' to eat at the canteen. Um . . .'

Specky suddenly remembered what Screamer had said, about how Robbo and Danny were quick to have him kicked out of the team. Why did they believe that he had turned against them?

'What?' he said.

As cruel as Robbo and Danny had been to him recently, Specky hoped this conversation was the first small step to being mates again. Maybe Robbo was about to say he had been wrong and he was sorry.

'What? You were going to say something else?' pressed Specky.

'Yeah, did you come to my house yesterday? Dad said he thought he saw you.'

Specky was disappointed.

'I guess that could've been me,' he said as nonchalantly as he could. 'I was riding my bike around there, so it could've been – can't remember.'

'Oh, cool, okay,' mumbled Robbo. 'Catch ya later.'

As Specky kicked the footy with Johnny for the rest of morning recess, he was blissfully unaware that ten kilometres away in an office in the city, three men were talking about him.

'I really liked the game of the Johnson boy,' said Bob Stockdale, Grub's right-hand man and Chairman of Selectors for the Victorian team. 'He reminded me of a young Matthew Pavlich – big and strong, and what about that mark he took? It was a beauty.'

'Yeah, I liked him, too, Bobby,' replied Grub in his gravelly voice. 'The old man's a bit of a worry, though. The way he cornered us after the game and kept telling us how good his son was. That bothers me a bit.'

'But that's not the kid's fault,' said Bob. 'You know better than anyone that there's always gonna be one or two of the parents who are pains in the neck, and try and push their kids up as hard as they can. If they knew they were doing more harm than good they might think twice about embarrassing themselves and their poor boys. I've heard about this guy through the local league they play in. He's been warned off a few times. I don't think we can let the fact that he acts like an idiot influence us when it comes to judging this kid, though.'

'I knew there was a reason I kept you around for twenty-one years, Bobby.' Grub grinned. 'You're right.'

In the corner of the room sat the newest member of the selection panel. Evan Dillon listened carefully to the two legends of junior football as they decided on their potential squad.

Evan was at least twenty years younger than Grub and Bob and he privately thought that they had been around for too long. It was time for a change, preferably with him as the new coach. As a result, Evan took every opportunity to disagree with them, and it was the source of some tension among the three.

'What about this Magee kid, Grub?' he enquired, with a defiant look in his eye. 'The way you were talking before the game, I was expecting to see a cross between Chris Judd and Warren Tredrea. From watching him play he's more like a cross between Bart and Homer Simpson. He didn't impress me one bit, and I don't think there's any way he'll make the squad.'

Grub turned his chair around and fixed his gaze on Evan.

'Ahh, Evan,' he said. 'You learn, when you've been in this job as long as I have, not to judge a young player on just one performance. Remember the first player you recommended to us as a selector? He turned out to be the captain of a hockey team and was just filling in to make up the numbers. He'd never played a game of football before then, or since probably.'

Bob Stockdale choked on his coffee as he tried desperately not to laugh. Grub continued, as Evan Dillon turned a bright shade of red.

'I do agree that Magee didn't play well at all on the day. Not to mention the damage he did to my poor old Benz. It was very unlike him to play so selfishly, and you know that's one of my pet hates. But I've seen him half a dozen times over the past two years and his form, in particular in the Diadora Cup games, has been outstanding.'

Grub stood up from his chair and moved over to the window to watch the city traffic below.

'I'm not sure what was going on with him in the game against the Falcons. I do know that he left Gosmore Grammar recently. I wonder if that had anything to do with it. Bobby, make a few calls for me, will ya? I need to know what's going on with that kid. He can play, but we need him to find some form quickly, because there are a couple of hundred other kids who want to make this team as badly as he does.'

With that, the selectors moved on to discussing another bunch of aspiring hopefuls, with Specky's chances of making the prestigious Victorian squad very much hanging in the balance.

10. the three musketeers

After the drama of the last week, the next two days at school went by for Specky without much incident.

'Right, here we are. Now, you're sure you don't want me to come with you?'

Specky was sitting in the front passenger seat next to his dad. They were parked outside a cemetery. Specky had asked his parents if he could take the morning off from school to attend Danny's grandmother's funeral. He got out of the car.

'No, that's okay, Dad, you can go to your meeting. I'll be okay . . . but thanks.'

'Well, Danny's a good friend and it's great you wanna be there for him. Make sure you head back to school as soon as it's ended.'

Specky nodded and made his way toward Danny and his grieving relatives. He had never been to a funeral, or a burial for that matter. Well, technically he had, as a baby at his biological mother's service, but he couldn't remember that.

Specky gingerly stepped past a row of gravestones and quietly edged his way into the large group of mourners – mainly a sea of elderly Italian women dressed in black, many of whom were sobbing and comforting one another.

Specky spotted Danny, his parents, Uncle Joe, and the rest of his family at the front of the group – arm in arm, they stood around the coffin of Danny's grandmother and the grave. Specky hadn't spoken to them at the packed church as he and his dad had been hidden among friends and relatives in the back row.

Specky took a couple more steps toward the burial gathering. A priest was praying out loud in Italian while four large men proceeded to lower the coffin into the grave. Without warning, Danny's mother began to howl uncontrollably, which sparked off a wave of howling from other family members. Specky shuffled uncomfortably.

He had never experienced anything like this before. He was overcome with sadness as he watched Danny comfort his grieving parents. He couldn't help but think of his own family, and how much he loved them – even Alice – and his own problems suddenly seemed very insignificant compared to what he was seeing in front of him.

'Hey.'

Specky felt a nudge in his side. It was Robbo.

'Hey,' Specky whispered back, happy to see the big fella. And judging by the look on Robbo's face – both surprised and pleased at the same time – Specky could tell Robbo was happy to see him, too.

They stood side by side, without saying a word. They didn't have to. They were there for their mate.

It wasn't until the service had ended and everyone began to stream out of the cemetery that Danny caught sight of Specky and Robbo.

'I'm really sorry about your Nonna Nina,' said Specky, knowing Danny always referred to his grandmother as his *nonna*, the Italian word for grandmother.

For a moment Danny didn't say a word, and

Specky began to wonder if it had been a mistake for him to show up. His friend looked as though he had been crying, but he was holding it together and Specky couldn't tell if he was pleased to see him or not.

Suddenly, Danny flung his arms around Specky and Robbo, hugging them both tightly.

'You two are the best ma . . . s . . . tha . . . a guy . . . cod . . . hav . . .' he mumbled into Specky's shoulder, choking back tears.

'You're a good mate, too,' comforted Specky.

'Yeah, you are, and . . . yeah,' added Robbo, not quite sure what to say.

Danny pulled away from them and regained his composure.

'I'm sorry, Speck . . .' he sniffed.

Woah, thought Specky. He's at his grandmother's funeral and he's saying sorry to me for how he's treated me in the last week. Wow. That's big. Maybe Robbo will apologise too.

'I'm sorry I got snot on your jumper,' Danny said.

'What?'

Danny pointed at Specky's shoulder.

'I'm sorry that I got snot on your jumper,'

he repeated, sniffing and wiping tears from his face.

Suddenly Specky began to chuckle – mainly out of embarrassment. Danny wasn't thinking about their fight at all! He was more worried about his runny nose. Specky tried desperately to stop laughing – he was in a cemetery, after all!

'What did you think Danny was saying sorry about?' added Robbo.

'Oh . . .' croaked Danny, looking awkward.

For a moment Specky and his friends stared at each other. He knew that they had suddenly worked out that he was expecting an apology from them.

But it was too late, Specky was chuckling uncontrollably. And with all the raw emotion in the air, to Specky's surprise, Danny started to laugh as well – and so did Robbo.

Within moments, all three boys were guffawing loudly.

Some of Danny's relatives shot looks of disapproval in the boys' direction, but no one seemed seriously annoyed. Many, like Danny's father, were just happy to see Danny smile.

'Thank you for coming, you boys,' he said, stepping forward to shake Specky and Robbo's hands. 'Danny's lucky to have you two around. And it's great to see you all together again – like the Three Musketeers.'

Specky grinned. It wasn't the kind of reconciliation that he had imagined – there had been no fanfare or big gestures, just old friends supporting each other. And none of them had had to say anything. They knew they were all mates again.

'So, Josh, Simon,' continued Mr Castellino. 'You're welcome to come back to the house for something to eat and drink.'

'That would be nice, thanks,' said Robbo.

Before Specky could answer, something caught his eye. Looking past Mr Castellino, he saw a figure pass behind a tombstone at the very end of the cemetery. It was Screamer. Specky looked at Danny and Robbo – they hadn't seen him.

'So, will you be joining us?' Mr Castellino asked Specky again.

Specky politely declined and told Danny's father that he had to get back to school.

As he walked through the cemetery gates, Specky took Robbo aside.

'Did Screamer say he was coming today – to the funeral?' he asked.

'Nah, he couldn't make it, why?'

'No, reason. I'll catch ya later!'

Specky wondered why Screamer had come. Perhaps he had turned up to support Danny, but had been put off by seeing him there. Specky decided to go back and talk to him.

But when Specky arrived at the spot where Screamer had been standing, he was nowhere to be seen. Specky looked down to where his foot had caught on something. It was the wrapping on some freshly cut flowers. Specky crouched down. There was a card attached to it that simply said, *Happy Birthday, Craig.*

As Specky was standing up again, he glanced at the gravestone directly in front of him. It read:

Craig Johnson
A football legend in the making
Age 15
Loving son of Kevin and Fiona
and brother of Derek

11. text message

Back in class it was difficult for Specky to concentrate on his schoolwork.

Screamer didn't show up at all for school that day and he wasn't at footy training either.

Specky's mind went into overdrive about what he had found out. What had happened to Screamer's brother, Craig? There were so many things about Screamer that no one knew.

'Heads up, Speck!'

Specky looked up just in time to see Johnny drill the footy at him. He grabbed the ball easily and was about to kick it back when Coach Pate called the team over.

As it turned out, training that day ended up being a lot more fun than Specky had expected.

After feeling down about footy in general, and after going to the funeral that morning, Specky was surprised to realise that he was revelling in tackling, kicking and marking. And Specky's teammates seemed more receptive to him than they had been just a few days earlier. Maybe Screamer had talked to them. Or maybe the tension between Specky, Robbo and Danny had been affecting the whole team.

Either way, Specky knew that regardless of what was going on in the lives of AFL players, they had to put it all aside when it came to match day or training and just concentrate on the job at hand. He had found out the hard way that the moment your mind started to wander you ran the risk of compromising training for the rest of the team or, even worse, ruining the game plan on match day. For however long the game went, or the training session lasted, he had always been able to immerse himself in footy. This was, Specky thought, one of the reasons why he loved to play and train, and he couldn't believe he had let personal issues affect his chances of making the Victorian squad. Coach Pate seemed to share this philosophy, and she paid no attention to any of the matters that took place outside the football team. She played no favourites. As far as she was concerned, footy was footy and they were all there for the same reason: to improve their skills, develop their team work and to have fun. And that suited Specky just fine.

Beep Beep. Specky reached into his pocket and took out his mobile phone. He had a text message.

Hi. I think we should talk. Christina.

Specky re-read Christina's message several times before dialling her number. He didn't like the look of it.

'Hi. I just got your message. We just finished training and –'

'Speck,' said Christina's voice quietly, but firmly, on the other end.

'Yeah?'

'I think we should, um . . . maybe we should, um . . .'

Specky stopped walking. This wasn't sounding good. He had to say something quick.

'Look, I'm really sorry for the other night. I know you were only trying to help me,' he blurted out. 'It was unfair of me. And, by the way, I know all about Screamer's hidden talent.'

'You do?'

'Yeah, and well, I can understand why you didn't want to say anything. 'Cause his dad doesn't –'

'Well, great! Now *you* can use it against him!' Christina said, cutting Specky off.

'But that's what I'm trying to tell you,' said Specky. 'I'm not gonna use it against him. *You* were the one who was going to do that.'

Specky winced. He knew he shouldn't have said that.

'I know I was!' said Christina defensively. 'But then I had second thoughts. I was just trying to help you, but you didn't want my help anyway.'

The conversation wasn't turning out the way Specky wanted it to. Somehow it had turned into an exact repeat of the other night at the cinema.

'Look. I think it might be best if . . . um, you know, we break up, and just be friends.'

There. Christina had just said what Specky had dreaded the most.

'Speck?'

'Yeah. I heard ya.'

'So, I'll catch you later then?'

Specky wanted to yell out at the top of his lungs how much Christina meant to him. He even wanted to say the L word. The word he had never said to anyone else. He wanted to say all of this, but couldn't. He didn't.

'Yeah, see ya later.'

'Okay. Bye, Speck.'

'Bye.'

12. meanwhile . . . back at the game

'C'mon on, boys!' cheered some of the parents, as Specky and his Booyong High teammates ran out onto the visitors' oval for another Saturday morning footy match – this time against the Yardley College Magpies.

'Hey, Magee,' called Screamer as they jogged out to take their positions. 'Heard Christina came to her senses and dumped ya.'

Specky shook his head. News sure travelled fast around the school. But, of course, he had told Alice, and he should have realised that that would be like putting it on the evening news.

'Yeah, whatever,' shrugged Specky, trying to look like it didn't worry him.

Screamer snorted and sprinted off toward the

goal square. Normally, Specky would've been a lot more cheesed off by a remark like that, but since learning of Screamer's family secrets he couldn't help seeing his old rival in a different light.

Specky hadn't told anyone about Screamer's brother. He was curious to find out more himself, but knew Screamer wouldn't tell him. He wondered if Christina knew anything, but thinking about that just reminded him that he couldn't phone and ask her. He decided not to think about any of it for a while and just focus on footy.

'Have a good one, Speck!'

'Go, Speck!'

'Yeah, you too,' replied Specky to his teammates, who were definitely making him feel like part of the team again.

Specky gave the thumbs-up to Danny, who, surprisingly, had shown up to play that morning.

'Life has to go on. My nonna would've wanted me to play,' he had said to Specky earlier in the change rooms.

Danny wore some black tape around his arm in honour of his grandmother, and most of

Danny's closest friends, including Specky, did the same.

The umpire's whistle sounded the start of the game.

Specky had had a quiet chat with Coach Pate after training during the week. Like all good players, Specky took responsibility for his own performances, and after his poor game the previous week he had sought out the coach to try and work out what had gone wrong and how he could improve. They both agreed that the interrupted preparation coming into the game hadn't helped, and that Specky was feeling too much pressure to perform at the high standard that he set himself, straight away. Coach Pate had suggested that Specky play in a new position this week, as a challenge. Specky had jumped at the idea. He knew that he could play full-forward and centre half-forward, and had even played centre half-back a couple of times. Today, for the first time, he was going to line up on the wing. He recalled that St Kilda coach, Grant Thomas, had played Nick Riewoldt there on a couple of occasions during the past year, and if it was good enough for the Saints' star to play there, then it was going to be good enough for him.

'Finally! The coach has come to her senses. Magee shouldn't be anywhere near my boy. Hide him out on the wing where he won't get in the way of anyone.'

Specky didn't have to turn around. He recognised the voice. It was Screamer's dad, as always giving advice where it wasn't needed or wanted. Specky ignored him and made a promise to himself that, no matter what, he was going to enjoy today's game.

And enjoy it he did. Right from the opening bounce, things fell into place for Booyong High. It all started in the middle, where Robbo and Danny were back to their very best form. Danny, in particular, was playing a blinder.

A traumatic event, like the passing of a loved one, can lead to one of two outcomes. Either the player concerned struggles to concentrate and, understandably, doesn't have his mind on football, or he is inspired to new heights in an attempt to mark the occasion with an outstanding performance. Today, Danny reminded Specky of another one of his very favourite players, Brett Kirk from the Sydney Swans. Specky loved the way he played. He was totally fearless and as committed to his teammates as any footballer in the competition. Specky had read an article about Kirk and it said that his grandfather, Wally Moras, was a World War Two veteran who had been his inspiration over the years. It didn't surprise Specky – he thought that Kirk played in the true spirit of the 'Diggers' and it was one of the reasons he admired him so much. And today, Danny was doing a fair job of impersonating him. He was in and under every pack, burrowing for the ball and feeding it out by handball to his teammates running past. Once or twice Specky found himself just standing and watching Danny play, he was so in awe of his performance.

At quarter time, the Lions had kicked six goals to the oppositions one. There were smiles all round as they huddled together for Coach Pate. She didn't hold back on the praise for Danny.

'That was just inspiring, Danny. I know it's been a tough week, but you've shown so much character today.'

All of the boys shouted their encouragement and Specky slapped Danny on the back. He couldn't have been happier if the praise had been directed at him.

This is what footy's about, he thought as he

jogged back out to the wing.

It had been a pretty quiet first quarter for Specky, but that was more to do with the fact that the ball was coming straight out of the middle and going into their forward line. He hadn't really been needed.

'Stay patient,' he reminded himself. 'The opportunities will come.'

The wind had sprung up and was blowing to his side of the oval. The ball remained there for the majority of the quarter, and Specky all of a sudden found himself in the middle of the action. And he thrived on the chances he was given.

He attacked the first ball at full speed and picked up a difficult half volley that landed at his boot laces. In the same motion he fired off a beautiful handpass to the Bombay Bullet, who was streaming past.

Specky flung his body in front of a Magpie player who was giving chase, meeting him with a perfect hip-and-shoulder, shepherding him out of the way just in time to let the Bullet run on to kick a goal.

While celebrating the goal, Specky looked up and caught sight of Grub Gordan sitting high in the Yardley College grandstand. He saw him turn to the man sitting next to him.

'That's why the kid's one of the best, Evan,' Grub said, far out of Specky's hearing. 'We know he can take the high marks, but one of the things we want is for a player to have "clean hands", and I don't mean he washes them before he plays. What I mean is that the real good players rarely, if ever, fumble. That ball was really travelling and Magee was able to bend down, pick it up off his boot laces as clean as a whistle, and handball it into the hands of that midfielder before the kid knew what was happening.'

'It was an okay effort, I suppose,' conceded Evan, begrudgingly.

'What was just as impressive,' continued Grub. 'Was the fact that he was then able to shepherd that other kid away, allowing his teammate to go on and kick the goal. That says more to me than anything else. He thinks of the team and not just himself. I like it. I like it a lot.'

Grub settled back to watch Specky and his teammates completely dominate the next two quarters. Smashing Sols was charging through packs and laying the hard tackles, while Robbo constantly palmed the ball out of the ruck, right down the throat of Johnny – who continued to stack up the possessions.

'What the heck is all that yapping?' grumbled Grub, looking down the grandstand.

'It's some kid calling the game,' said Evan, also staring past his feet. 'And he's all set up with his card table, dictaphone and binoculars!'

And welcome back, folks. Ben 'Gobba' Higgins, former Booyong player and now full-time commentator extraordinaire here to bring you all the action, right here on Gobba Radio-slash-TV.

'Getta load of it! He's like a miniature Dennis Cometti,' laughed Grub. 'He's great!'

We are witnessing a clinical exhibition of football here today, folks. I'm not sure what Coach Pate said to her players this week, but, by golly, I haven't seen them combine this well for many a day.

The ball is thrown in on the Magpies half-forward line, with the Booyong Lions in complete control by fifty-three points, well into the third quarter. Roberts flips the ball over the back into the arms of WHO ELSE BUT CASTELLINO. The Italian Stallion is having a field day, running around his opponent like he isn't even there! The boy had better get rid of that ball or he'll get leather poisoning.

Grub smiled and chuckled, while Evan rolled his eyes.

Castellino kicks across his body to the outer wing where the ball finds Simon Magee, one out with his opponent. Oh, it hardly seems fair, folks. Magee brushes him aside easily and, oh no, the Magpie scumbag has kicked out and tried to trip him. Magee looks like he's going down . . . but, no, he regains his footing and sprints off down the ground. He's got the grace and balance of a gazelle, that lad. The move out to the wing has been an inspired one. The Magpies just haven't got a player who can match him in the air or on the ground. Look at him go! Johnny Cockatoo has made position on the flank, but Magee ignores him and looks further

118

*afield. He puts boot to ball and it's a sizzling daisy-
cutter of a pass, right onto the chest of Big Bad
Bustling Screamer Johnson – the new Barry Hall!*

*Johnson has been pretty good today and is lining up
for his fourth goal, but, gee, the way the ball is being
delivered I reckon I would have kicked six or seven out
there today. Johnson runs in and drills home his fourth
for the day and the Lions are further ahead.*

At the end of the game Specky and his teammates clip-clopped into the change rooms, happy
with their outstanding victory.

'Well, if that performance hasn't won Derek a
spot in the final trial match for the State team,'
said Screamer's dad, his eyes popping out of his
leathery tanned face, 'then the whole bloody
thing must be rigged.'

'Thank you, Mr Johnson,' said Coach Pate,
not impressed. 'Boys, that was a superb performance. Some of you may already be aware of this,
but the Coach of the Victorian Under Fifteen
team was here today, along with another of the
selectors, and they would like to have a word.
Please welcome Coach Jay Gordan and Evan
Dillon.'

Specky gulped as a hush came over the room. Grub Gordan, with Evan by his side, walked in like a cowboy from an old western movie stepping into a saloon.

'Boys, good effort today. You worked together pretty well. Castrati, fantastic game!'

Specky caught Danny turning red, obviously just holding off from pointing out to Mr Gordan that he had got his name horribly wrong.

'As you know, we have a final trial game coming up to pick our Victorian Under Fifteen team,' said Grub. 'This may be the biggest game any of you boys have played in, but it's not the be all and end all. Heaps of players who didn't make the State team have still gone on to play AFL.'

A pause followed.

'But it is a damn big honour,' he added in a deep booming voice.

Specky held his breath as Grub Gordan took in another one.

'I am pleased to announce that Simon Magee and Derek Johnson have made it into the squad of forty from which the State team will be picked. Training begins next week. Come prepared and good luck! And you . . .'

Grub turned to Gobba who was standing in the doorway of the change rooms.

'You give my secretary a call. Dennis Cometti is a good mate of mine and I reckon he would like to hear your recording of the game.'

Grub Gordan slipped his business card into Gobba's hand.

As the Victorian selectors left the building, Specky's teammates erupted into whoops and whistles – congratulating him and Screamer . . . and Gobba.

13. state of mind

When Specky got to school on Monday morning, he discovered that his and Screamer's selection for the final trial game had made *The Booyong High Bugle*'s headlines in a rushed one-page special edition.

BOOYONG BOYS MAKE FINAL STATE TRIAL – A SPECKY SURPRISE FOR SOME!

By Theresa Fallon

The Bugle just got word that two of Booyong High's football champions have been selected to play in the final trial game from which the Victorian Under 15 State team will be chosen. Year 9 students Derek 'Screamer' Johnson and Simon 'Specky' Magee have been given the opportunity of a lifetime – the chance to prove that they're good enough to make the team. The all-important match will be played at the end of term, on July 8.

While yours truly expected Johnson to be selected – he starred all season for Booyong – the inclusion of Magee is something of a surprise.

His first game back after his banishment from Gosmore Grammar was, let's be kind, not vintage Magee, although his reputation and talent over the years is still, so it seems, something that cannot be easily overlooked. I am told he played more like the Magee of old on the weekend, but we must take into account the fact that the opposition was the lowly Yardley Magpies.

So only time will tell if Magee will rise to the occasion. Not just in the games ahead for our beloved Lions, but perhaps for the entire State as well. Watch this space!

Annoyed, Specky shoved the school newspaper into his locker.

'Hey, legend!'

It was the Great McCarthy.

'Hey, what are you doing here?' asked Specky, knowing that Year 12s rarely ventured into the area of the school where the Year 7s to 9s hung out.

'Just wanted to let you know that we're having a party after the deb ball at my house – so you and Tiger Girl are invited.'

'Thanks, and . . . ?'

'And what?'

'Well, you could've told me that anytime. Or told Alice to tell me. So, what else is there?

Specky knew that Dieter had something on his mind, judging from the way he was swaying and chewing on his bottom lip.

'Look,' he said, taking a deep breath, 'I'm packing myself about this deb ball. You saw me try to do the Boston Two Step. I moved more like a Boston Bun.'

'Don't worry about it! Just go with the flow. It's early days,' reassured Specky.

The Great McCarthy still looked upset.

'Look, maybe, you should talk to Alice. She'll understand if you want to pull out. There are four weeks of practice to go. She can still try to find someone else to be her partner. But then again she'd be behind everyone else while her new partner tries to learn to dance. And she'll hate your guts and probably won't talk to you ever again and . . .' Specky trailed off sadly, thinking about how Christina wasn't talking to him either.

'Yeah, yeah, okay! I get it!' said Dieter shaking his head. 'I'll catch ya later.'

'Hey!' Specky called after him. 'Did you see the article in the school newspaper? That Full On chick got stuck into me again.'

'Don't worry about it. Just go with the flow.'

Specky grinned. He figured he deserved to have his own line thrown back at him. But he decided that, as daggy as it sounded, he was going to go with his own advice anyway. For the next month, Specky would do just that – go with the flow.

It was the first time in a while that Specky was able to get back into a normal everyday routine, without all the extra drama he had become accustomed to. He went to school, hung out with Danny and Robbo again, played footy on Saturdays for Booyong High, continued to go to deb practice with Tiger Girl, and attended training sessions for the Victorian squad. If only he and Christina hadn't fought, things would be perfect, he thought. But he tried to put that out of his mind.

The first Victorian squad training session was terrifying, intense and exciting all at the same time.

'Hurry up, boys.' Grub Gordan waved them over.

Specky joined his State trial teammates in a huddle, fully expecting a gruelling training session. Specky noticed Screamer looking more agitated than usual. He held his head low and kept kicking the back of his left heel with his right foot. Specky turned to see Mr Johnson on the boundary with some other parents, glaring at Screamer more like a hawk than a proud father. Specky still hadn't mentioned anything about Screamer's piano-playing or his brother. To avoid creating any sort of hassle, Specky had decided it was best to keep out of it and say nothing at all to anyone.

'Right, boys, now is the time to show us what you've got,' barked Grub.

'Have a look around ya. I'm sure you recognise some of the faces here, but there are others that you would never have laid eyes on. There are forty boys here from all over the State of Victoria. And I don't want to hear one word of whinging from you city boys, either. You're lucky we're training in your own backyard. Magee, how long did it take you to get 'ere?'

'How long?' asked Specky, suddenly aware that everyone had turned their stares on him.

'Yeah, how long? What, don't you understand English, son?'

A couple of the boys laughed nervously, silently thankful that it wasn't them that was being questioned.

'Well . . . umm . . . arrr,' stuttered Specky.

'Look, it's not a hard question,' growled Grub, a little louder. 'How long did it take you to get from your home to the Punt Road Oval?'

'Oh, right,' Specky replied, hurriedly doing a quick calculation. 'It took about twenty-five minutes.'

'Okay. Edwards, how long did it take you to get here?'

'About six and a half hours, Coach,' answered Brian Edwards, a star centreman from the town of Mildura in Victoria's far north.

'And what about you, Molopolous?'

'Took us about five and a half hours, but me dad did get a bit lost,' said the tall young ruckman from Orbost, down in the south-eastern corner of the State.

This broke the ice, and even Grub managed a smile.

'Well, what I'm saying is that we have all made some sacrifices to be here today, and yet none of you have got any guarantees that you'll make the team. That will depend on how you perform on the training track today and at the final trial game in a few weeks' time. So, don't hold anything back.'

With that, the players were taken away to do their warm-ups. Some of these kids looked huge to Specky and as he was jogging alongside Spiro Molopolous, he could've sworn that Spiro had a three-day growth on his chin.

Training soon got underway and the first thing

Specky noticed was the speed and intensity of each of the drills. The ball zinged around during the various handball and kicking drills, rarely hitting the ground.

Specky was a little tentative at first, but he soon picked up the pace and he was absolutely loving the fact that when he called for the ball, it was almost always delivered to him perfectly, lace out and on the chest.

He was eager to impress and when Brian Edwards got the ball in his hands, Specky called out loudly and led hard out toward where the coaches were standing.

Brian was a superstar, and his reputation had even made its way to Melbourne. He swung onto his left foot and delivered the most magnificent, low drop punt that Specky had ever seen. He was almost smiling as the ball approached him, but then he realised it was coming a lot quicker than he had anticipated. With the eyes of the whole selection panel on him, Specky decided to take the mark on his chest, just to make extra sure that he didn't drop the ball.

It thudded safely into his body and he wrapped his arms around the footy.

Specky quickly played on, preparing to kick the ball to the next group of players when he heard a noise that sounded like a sick coyote on its death bed. Only, it was screaming his name.

'MAAAGGGGEEEEEE, WHAT IN THE HELL DO YOU THINK YOU ARE DOING?'

The training drill ground to a halt as Grub Gordan waddled towards Specky with a fierce scowl on his face.

'I could have picked a thousand kids who could come and train here today and run around and take baby chest marks, just to play it safe. That's not what we want to see, son. We don't want you to take the easy, safe option. TEST YOUR-SELF, BOY! YOU CAN DO BETTER! I don't ever want to see you take a chest mark again, unless we're playing on a ground that is ten feet underwater and the rain is coming down sideways.'

Specky remained frozen, not even daring to blink.

'And even then, I'm not sure I want you to take a chest mark. TAKE THE BALL OUT IN FRONT – IN YOUR HANDS! I don't care if you drop it, as long as you drop it trying to do the right thing. Take it in the hands. It's harder for the defender to punch the ball away, and it's easier and quicker for you to give off a handball if the ball is already in ya big bloody mitts. Do you understand me?'

'Got it!' croaked Specky, his heart pumping out of control.

'Right! Off ya go then.'

Specky's ears were burning as he ran to the back of the group.

There goes my chance of making the team, he thought, but he soon learned that if every player that Grub Gordan took aside and laid down the law to was disqualified, then there'd be no one left in the team. And it had been good advice.

Specky felt a little better when Screamer copped a spray from Grub for slipping over during one of the drills.

'What good are ya to anyone on the ground?' he roared. 'Weak players go to ground. Don't you be weak on me again!'

Specky noticed Screamer shaking his head, upset with himself. But Grub wasn't finished.

'Don't take it personally, Johnson. If I didn't care, and didn't think you could play, I wouldn't waste my breath,' he added, before turning his attention to another player.

After ninety minutes of some of the most intense and exhaustive training Specky had ever experienced, the session came to an end. Instead of just wandering off to get changed, though, they were all made to do a thorough warm-down session, stretching muscles that Specky didn't even know he had.

Finally, with the daylight fading and muscles aching, Specky and his teammates made their way back to the change rooms.

'Hey, Magee, where do you think you're going?'

Specky closed his eyes and thought, what now?

But he slowly turned to find Brian Edwards, grinning – still with a football in hand.

'I reckon there's still at least twenty-five minutes before the sun goes down. I wouldn't mind doing a bit of extra work on my non-preferred foot, and I reckon you could do with some practice taking those marks in your hands.'

Specky looked at him, not sure whether he was having a go or not.

'Grub's the best junior coach in the country, mate. We're all lucky to be learning from him. When he speaks, we should all listen. My older brother played in the Victorian Under Fifteen side three years ago, under him. I've known him for a while now. All he wants is for us to be the best players we can be.'

While Specky could see that many people would think Brian took himself a little too seriously, there was something he liked about him. He was cocky and confident, but not in an arrogant way.

'Come on, we're losing the light. You get up there, about thirty metres away, and just run at me, flat out. I'll try and drill them at your chest and you take them in the hands.'

Specky jogged the distance and for the next twenty minutes led at Brian until the light disappeared and it was impossible to see.

'I kicked forty-four balls at you,' said Brian. 'Six of them missed you altogether, which was my fault, and of the other thirty-eight, you marked thirty-one of them cleanly into your hands. Nice work!'

'Why did you keep score?' asked Specky, amazed that Brian could recall all of that.

'Well, how am I going to know if I improve next time?'

Specky could tell that this was going to become an after-training ritual.

As the sunset dipped and the first stars appeared in the crisp early evening sky, the boys strolled off the oval toward their waiting dads.

'Thanks for doing a bit of extra work, mate,' said Specky.

'No worries,' grinned Brian. 'I'm looking forward to the trial match in a couple of weeks. I've always dreamed of wearing a Big V jumper. Hopefully we're on the same side. I reckon we would work together pretty well.'

'Yeah, I think so too,' Specky replied, smiling back. 'Well, I better get going, Mum will wonder where Dad and I have got to. We usually eat dinner at six-thirty.'

'That'd be nice,' said Brian, as he made his way over to his father, sitting on the bonnet of the family wagon. 'We won't be home until at least one-thirty in the morning.'

'You're kidding!' Specky said. 'That long – seriously?'

'Yeah, but I don't care. I want to play professional footy more than anything. Dad's making me read school books all the way down and all the way back so I don't fall behind, but I'll probably sleep for the last two or three hours tonight. Anyway, I'll see you soon. And don't forget, take 'em in the hands.'

Specky didn't stop talking about his training experience all the way home. His father nearly swerved off the road when he told him that some of the other players in the squad, like Brian, had a six-and-a-half hour drive ahead of them.

'I will never complain about taking you to training again,' promised Mr Magee as they pulled into the driveway at home.

14. footballer's mush

At the end of the following day, after the school bell had sounded, Specky weaved his way through the hordes of students streaming out of the Booyong High grounds.

'Wait up, Speck!' It was Tiger Girl. 'I've got something to tell ya.'

Tiger Girl's face beamed as she ran up alongside Specky.

'I've decided to have a party after the deb at my place,' she said.

'But I thought it was gonna be at –'

'At McCarthy's place. Yeah, it was, but his folks weren't keen 'cause they're renovating the house or something. Anyway, the Year Eleven girls are organising their own party in the city somewhere

136

and the Year Ten girls are splitting up and having their own individual parties. So I thought I'd have a small one at my place. Unfortunately, Mum said I have to invite parents, so let your folks know. And you can invite Christina, if you like, too.'

Specky was taken aback. Why would Tiger Girl say that when she knew they had broken up? Had she forgotten?

'Um, I'm not going out with her anymore, remember?' he said.

'Yeah, I know, but this might be your chance to try and get back together again.'

'Who said I want to get back together with her?' said Specky, even though that's all he had thought about since they had broken up.

'C'mon!' said Tiger Girl. 'I've seen you in class, staring into space, thinking about her.'

'Yeah, right!' Specky scoffed.

'Don't "yeah, right" me! I know you, Speck. There's two things you always think about – footy and Christina. Or both at the same time.'

Tiger Girl was right. Specky hadn't been able to stop thinking about Christina during the past few weeks and had wondered the whole time how he could make it up to her.

'You two were so cute together. Why did you break up?'

Specky hadn't really told anyone why he and Christina had separated. Why would he? He just had to get over it and get on with life. But after some nonstop coaxing from Tiger Girl, he decided to tell her – but he was vague about the details and didn't mention Screamer.

'Well, it's clear what you have to do now, isn't it?' she said, after hearing the story. 'You have to do something for her, to win her back. Something that would be a big deal for you to do.'

'Like buy her flowers or something?' said Specky.

Tiger Girl rolled her eyes.

'Oh, yeah, that would really work,' she said sarcastically. 'No! It has to be something personal. Something that proves you're a good guy.'

Specky looked at Tiger Girl blankly. He wasn't cut out for all this mushy relationship stuff.

She continued.

'And it has to be something that's not about you, a really big gesture. Like, helping someone she cares about, or fixing something. Something she'd be impressed by. You have to show you did it 'cause you care for her. And that you appreciate her trying to help you. 'Cause that's all she was trying to do.'

Suddenly Specky knew what he had to do. Tiger Girl had given him the perfect idea.

15. tell me

An hour after he had spoken to Tiger Girl, Specky slowly approached Screamer's house. He was feeling less sure of himself the closer he got.

So, this is my big plan? Talking Screamer into calling Christina? he thought nervously. She's obviously really upset about not being friends with him because of me, but I hope I don't make it worse . . . What am I doing? I must be bonkers!

Then he stepped onto the driveway, and heard Mr Johnson's voice booming from the open front windows. Specky was tempted to just turn around and leave.

But then he thought of Christina and steeled himself – he could always tell Screamer's dad he had come to talk to Screamer about the State trial game or something.

But as Specky walked closer to the house he could also hear Mrs Johnson's voice. Specky stopped. Screamer's parents were in the middle of an argument.

'Don't give me that rubbish,' shouted Mr Johnson. 'You're hiding something from me and I bloody well wanna know what's going on. Why did you say Derek might not be able to make the selection game?'

'Look, I don't know what I was thinking,' said Screamer's mum, in a quieter voice. 'And do you have to shout? Derek will come home and hear us fighting. The whole neighbourhood will hear us.'

'I don't care who hears us! What could you or Derek have possibly planned to do on that day that would take him away from the greatest opportunity he's ever had?'

Specky instantly put two and two together.

I bet that piano audition is on the same day! he thought.

'We haven't planned anything,' replied Mrs Johnson. 'But if we had, would it be so bad if he missed one game? There might be more to life than football, you know.'

There was a long pause. Specky could only imagine the shocked and angry expression on Mr Johnson's face.

'You've got some nerve,' hissed Screamer's dad.

'*I* have a nerve?' Mrs Johnson snapped back. Then her voice wavered. 'Kevin, you've got to back off. Derek is not Craig!'

There was another long silence.

'Whatever you're up to, you can drop it! This kid is going to be a football star – and I'm not going to let you ruin that for him or me. This has nothing to do with Craig.'

'No? Four years on and you still can't take yourself to visit his gravesite – not even for his birthday.'

Now Mrs Johnson sounded as though she was crying.

It was obvious to Specky that Screamer wasn't home and it wasn't the best moment to make himself known anyway. He would come back at another time.

Quietly he took a few steps backwards. As

Specky turned around, he was startled to find Screamer standing directly in front of him.

Specky wasn't sure how long Screamer had been standing there. His stare was frozen – his eyes bloodshot, close to tears. His mouth was tight-lipped and his breathing was heavy. Any second now Specky was expecting a right hook to the face, but there was nothing, not even a word. Then, to Specky's surprise and relief, Screamer just stepped aside and let Specky walk past. He kept walking and didn't look back once. He walked all the way home, shocked by what had just happened.

16. deb ball

'Wow, look at you!' beamed Mrs Magee proudly, as she looked to the top of the staircase.

Specky was smartly decked out in a black suit, bowtie, cufflinks and polished black shoes. The big night had arrived. In a couple of hours' time, he and Alice were to show their dance moves at this year's Booyong High deb ball.

'Hooley Dooley! Mr Dapper, come on down!' teased Mr Magee, who was also wearing his finest, and was pointing a camera in Specky's direction.

Specky grinned, swaggering down the stairs as if he were James Bond.

It's like I'm off to the Brownlow, he thought.

'Alice!' Mrs Magee called out. 'Dieter will be

here soon. You sure you don't want my help?'

'Help?' echoed Alice from her bedroom. 'No!'

'Woah, Mum, you look great,' said Specky, suddenly noticing that his mother was all dressed up in a black evening dress.

'Thank you, darling,' she said. 'Even with my belly?'

Specky nodded. His mother was six months pregnant and her belly was getting bigger by the week. The Magees had decided not to find out the sex of the baby until it was born, but Specky didn't care if it was a boy or a girl, he just couldn't wait for the day when he'd teach his younger sibling how to kick a footy.

Ding, dong.

Someone was at the front door. Mr Magee opened it to see the Great McCarthy standing there, also in a suit.

'Ah, another penguin,' Mr Magee joked.

'Hi, Mr M,' said Dieter, stepping inside. 'Is Alice ready? My folks are waiting in the car.'

'Dieter, you look so handsome,' said Mrs Magee. 'I think it's so great the boys are going to pick up the girls and arrive at the ball together. Just like the good old days.'

Specky made a face at Dieter, but he didn't respond. Specky could see beads of sweat on his forehead. He looked very nervous.

'Alice!' yelled Mr Magee. 'Your date is here.'

'Okay. Hold on!'

A few moments later Alice appeared at the top of the staircase.

There was a collective gasp.

Specky had never seen his sister so dressed up before. With her hair done up, and make-up expertly applied, she looked like a model. She swished down the stairs in her long flowing white dress.

Specky's dad clicked away with his camera, while his mother gushed.

'Darling, you look so beautiful! Doesn't she, Simon?'

'Oh, yeah, she scrubs up okay,' stirred Specky.

'Nick off,' snapped Alice, in a very unlady-like voice.

'I can't believe this is my little girl,' smiled Mr Magee. 'Dieter, what have you got to say?'

Specky moved aside to let the Great McCarthy step forward. Dieter was speechless.

'Well?' prompted Mr Magee.

'She's hot,' mouthed Dieter, his gaze fixed on Alice.

'Sorry?' said Mr Magee.

Specky snorted. And Alice winced and smiled at the same time.

'I mean, she's amazing. She's beautiful,' Dieter said, quickly correcting himself. 'Here, this is for you.'

The Great McCarthy handed Alice a corsage, which reminded Specky to grab his for Tiger Girl.

In no time at all, Specky and his parents were on their way to Tiger Girl's house. Alice headed directly to the ball with Dieter and the McCarthys.

'Wow!' choked Specky, when Tiger Girl appeared at the door.

She looked stunning. Specky hardly recognised her. He was so used to seeing her dressed casually, always wearing her tattered old Tigers scarf, with her hair looking as if she had just gotten out of bed. Now he had to do a double-take. With her hair up, her face glowing, lipstick on and make-up around her eyes, she looked like a princess. Specky nervously handed her the corsage.

'Mum, Specky's here. I'll see you at the hall,' she yelled back over her shoulder. 'You look great, Speck, and thanks for this.'

In the car, Tiger Girl handed Specky a gift. Mrs Magee smiled in the front seat.

'What's this for?' asked Specky.

'It's tradition for the debutante to give her partner a little present. To say thanks. So, thanks.'

Specky ripped open the gift. It was a book – the latest Hanger McPherson novel.

'Thought you might like it. I love them.'

'Cool. Thanks,' beamed Specky.

When they reached Booyong High's hall there was a buzz of excitement that filled the crisp night air. As parents headed inside to be seated, the debutantes and their partners gathered backstage.

'Okay, okay, try to keep the noise down everyone,' ordered Mrs Twiddle, who, in a shimmering sparkly red dress, resembled a giant Christmas ornament.

She ran around with a clipboard, ticking off couples as they arrived. Mr Twiddle followed a few steps behind, complimenting everyone on how elegant they looked.

'Woah, this is pretty full on, isn't it?' said Specky, who had started to feel a few butterflies.

'Yeah, I'm so excited,' grinned Tiger Girl, her eyes darting all over the place, checking out how the other girls were dressed. 'I'm just gonna duck into the toilets – last minute make-up check.'

Tiger Girl took off with some of her friends. Specky moved toward the stage curtain and peeked through. The hall was as dressed up as the debutantes were. Large tables covered in white cloths lined the edges of the dance floor (which was actually Booyong High's basketball court) and the walls and ceiling were adorned with metallic blue and silver balloons and fairy lights.

In the far back corner was a six-piece band. Shirley, the rehearsal pianist, was on one of the tables closest to the stage, dressed in her finest, chewing peanuts and sipping a drink. She seemed to be enjoying having the night off.

Specky spotted his folks talking to some of the other parents and was hit by another wave of butterflies.

But he wasn't as nervous as the Great McCarthy.

'Oh, man. I've just been to the loo twice and this tie is choking me,' he croaked. 'I don't know if I can do this.'

'What d'ya mean, you don't know?' asked Specky.

'The steps,' he said. 'Is it one, two, one for the Boston Two Step, or one, one, two? Oh, crap! I know I'm gonna stuff it up.'

Specky couldn't believe it. The Great McCarthy – a Year 12 student, admired by so many people at the school for being one of the coolest dudes around – was falling to pieces right before his very eyes.

'Look, you'll be fine. You were okay at rehearsals. Just enjoy it,' said Specky, trying his best to calm him down.

'I don't think I'm gonna be fine. Mate, I have a real phobia about this,' he said, taking a deep breath. 'There's only one thing for me to do.'

'You can't do a runner, if that's what you're

thinking,' snapped Specky. 'You can't do that to Alice.'

The Great McCarthy didn't answer. He just looked around frantically and darted off.

'Attention please, everyone,' announced Mrs Twiddle.

The debutantes and their partners shuffled in around her.

'Just a reminder – as we rehearsed it last Sunday. Girls will wait in the wings stage right, boys, stage left. The debutantes will be introduced in alphabetical order. Then their partners will be called out.'

Specky caught Tiger Girl smiling at him in anticipation. He also saw the Great McCarthy come out of the toilets, stop, then do a complete turn around and go back in.

Mrs Twiddle continued.

'Together you will meet in the centre of the stage, hold for a couple of seconds, then proceed, hand in hand, down the steps onto the dance floor. From there, you will walk down the middle of the floor toward the dignitaries' table at the far end of the hall. Remember not to rush. Take your time and smile. Once you reach the dignitaries, ladies will curtsy and gents bow. Then make your way to the starting position I gave you.'

Specky leant in to Tiger Girl.

'This is more intense than the pre-game rev-up speech we'd get from the coach before a Grand Final,' he whispered.

'And,' Mrs Twiddle said, taking a big breath. 'Once the last couple has come down, prepare for the Pride of Erin. Wait for the musicians and my cue to begin. Finally, have a great time. Nigel and I have loved getting to know you all and think you are beautiful young adults. We really do. Oh, I better stop now or I'm going to get emotional. Have fun, everyone!'

Everyone applauded and rushed to get into place. This was the moment. The curtains pulled back to reveal Mrs Twiddle moving downstage to the far-left corner. The parents and friends seated at their tables clapped and cheered loudly. Mrs Twiddle welcomed everyone and said a few words into the microphone.

'Have you seen Dieter?'

It was Alice, tugging at Specky's arm. She looked distraught.

'Where is he?' she asked nervously. 'I've been waiting for him to come out of the toilets. So I can wish him luck. But he hasn't come out. Then one of the boys told me he wasn't in there, so where the –'

'Look, it's okay,' said Specky.

'It's not okay, where is he?' Alice panicked. 'Mrs Twiddle's just started to announce the couples.'

Specky could only think the worst: Dieter's fears had finally got the better of him and he had bolted.

'I'll go and find him. He'll be around some-where. Don't worry,' he said to his sister, as if there was nothing to be concerned about. 'Just go and wait on your side of the stage. You won't be called for a while yet.'

Specky dashed to the very back of the hall, behind where the drama props and sets were stored, and out through a service door. He could hear Mrs Twiddle introducing the first couple.

'Miss Suzette Amsterdam, to be partnered by Mr Mark Adams.'

Loud applause echoed as Specky made his way outside.

'Dieter!' he called out. 'Dieter, where are you?'

The Great McCarthy was nowhere to be seen. Specky headed back inside.

'Our next couple,' continued Mrs Twiddle.

Specky made his way into the toilets.

'Dieter? You in here?'

All the stall doors were open, except for one.

'Dieter, are you there?' Specky banged on the closed toilet door.

'Yeah,' came a grunt from the other side of the door.

'What are you doing? My sister's freaking out. Come on! We're on soon.'

'Speck. I know this is hard for you to understand. But I think I'm having a panic attack or something. I can't go out and embarrass myself or Alice.'

'But if you don't do it you'll embarrass Alice anyway. She'll be gutted – in front of everyone. You don't want that to happen, do you?'

Specky waited for a reply. He heard a lot of shuffling noises.

'Dieter? What are you doing?' he asked.

'There's only one way I can go through with

154

this. And that's if I don't do it as me,' said the Great McCarthy.

'What? What are you talking about?'

Specky was totally confused.

Suddenly the stall door opened. Specky stumbled backward, startled by what he saw. The Great McCarthy was dressed in a tiger costume.

17. no way!

'What the . . . ?' gulped Specky.

'This is the only way I can go out there,' mumbled Dieter through the mouthpiece of the tiger costume.

'You gotta be kidding!' said Specky in utter disbelief. 'Where did you get it and how?'

'It's the old Tigers mascot costume I used to wear for Richmond. I threw it in the boot before picking up Alice.'

'I can see what it is,' remarked Specky, shaking his head. 'But you're not seriously gonna go out there wearing that? Are you?'

'I have no other choice. This is the only way I can overcome my fears.'

Specky had a flash of Alice, Mrs Twiddle and

everyone else reacting to the Richmond Tiger strolling out onto the stage.

'This is not on, mate,' said Specky. He knew he would have to take drastic steps. 'There's no way you can do this. You're gonna stuff up the whole deb for all the girls. It'll be a huge joke!'

'Yeah – like the joke's on you now you mean?' snorted Dieter, taking the tiger head off.

'What?' said Specky.

'The joke's on you, legend,' repeated Dieter, pulling out a digital camera and snapping a photo of Specky's horrified face.

Dieter was grinning from ear to ear. 'Alice, are you there?'

Alice popped her head into the boys' toilets.

'Yeah, I'm here.' She laughed loudly. 'I had the door open a little so I heard everything. We gotcha, squirt!'

Specky was stunned. He had been totally stooged.

'But, but you were freaking out about dancing long before you even knew I was going to the deb with Tiger Girl,' stuttered Specky, trying to make some sense of it.

'Yeah, I know. I *was* worried in the beginning,

but then, after a few rehearsals, I just faked it whenever I saw you. Alice keeps going on to me about how ya always stir her and how you said she'd have to get up early to catch you out. Well, we caught you out big-time, dude! You should see your face right now.' He turned the camera around. 'Check this out – here it is! Classic!'

Dieter and Alice roared with laughter.

'So, you've been planning it all this time?' asked Specky.

'Yep,' said Alice in between fits of laughter.

Dieter took off the Tiger costume. He was wearing his suit underneath.

'You guys are demented, you know that?' huffed Specky, as Dieter joined Alice.

'Yeah, we know,' said the Great McCarthy, halfway out of the toilets. 'But you'll get over it. Some bloke once gave me a good piece of advice – "Just go with the flow". See ya out there!'

It wasn't until well into the evening, after every debutante and their partner had been presented and they had performed the dances on the program, that Specky could crack a smile and even laugh a little at his sister and Dieter's joke.

'No hard feelings, legend? You know you can borrow my tiger costume anytime you want,' the Great McCarthy said to Specky, as he and Alice waltzed by for the hundredth time.

'They're not gonna let you forget it, are they?' said Tiger Girl, arm in arm with Specky, swirling around on the dance floor.

'Nah, but that's cool. I'll get 'em back one day.'

'Well, I've got something that will cheer you up – a surprise later on, at my party,' smiled Tiger Girl.

'What is it?' asked Specky.

'You'll see!'

When the ball ended, the debutantes went off to various after-parties. Many of the Year 11 girls and their partners had their own function planned in the city, while the Year 10s broke off into two groups and one group headed over to Tiger Girl's house.

'What are you guys doing here?' asked Specky, surprised to see Dieter and Alice. 'I thought you were off to the party in the city.'

'We are. But I promised TG we'd hang here for a while,' said Alice, reaching for some crackers and dip.

About twelve of the students showed up at Tiger Girl's home, all changed out of their formal wear and back in casual clothes. Most of them hung out listening to music in the lounge room at the front of the house, while the parents, including Mr and Mrs Magee, gathered separately in the kitchen and in a room leading out into the backyard.

'Don't forget. There's a surprise soon,' winked Tiger Girl. 'Hey, Alice, I wanna show you those cool pillows I got for my bedroom.'

'What surprise?' asked the Great McCarthy, as the girls left the room.

'Dunno,' shrugged Specky.

'Wake up, legend,' Dieter smirked.

'What?'

'She's into you, man! Are you blind?'

'Nah, she's not. It's Tiger Girl. We're just good mates.'

'Yeah, right, that's a good one. Take it from someone who knows, Speck, she's into you big-time!' For a moment Specky thought that Dieter was playing another joke on him and any second now Alice and Tiger Girl would appear laughing their heads off. But he wasn't. He was deadly serious.

'Really?' Specky asked, still doubtful.

'Yeah, really. I bet the surprise is she's gonna lay the big pash on ya.'

'The big what?'

'C'mon, legend. I know you're only in Year Nine, but you're not that gullible. She wants to lock lips with you, dude. The big smoocharoony – now that you're a single man and Christina's not around.

'Look,' he continued. 'You don't wanna be caught out and seem clueless. In fact, if you don't wanna look like an idiot who has no idea, you gotta make the first move.'

'What?' choked Specky.

'Yeah, you've gotta kiss her first. That's what she probably expects. They're probably out there talking about it now. You can't be a wimp.'

'But we're just mates. I don't think of her that way.'

'But look at her! She's a babe!'

Specky thought about Tiger Girl. She was beautiful, and she was one of his best mates.

'You can work out all the other details later,' Dieter pressed on. 'But you don't wanna be caught out and look like a loser or offend her.'

'Um, I'm not so sure about this . . .'

'Speck. I'm only telling you this 'cause you're my girlfriend's brother and I like ya. I don't need to be here at some lame party hanging around with a bunch of Year Tens. So, you can take my advice or leave it.'

Specky didn't get a chance to answer Dieter. The girls had returned.

'Speck,' said Tiger Girl, pulling him away. 'Can I talk to you?'

'The surprise?' asked Specky.

Tiger Girl nodded. Specky looked back over his shoulder to see the Great McCarthy nod and wink at him. Specky's heart was racing a hundred miles an hour – as if he had made a sudden lead to sprint away from a full-back. His palms were sweaty all of a sudden, and his mouth was so dry he didn't think he was going to be able to talk.

Tiger Girl dragged Specky into the hallway.

'Um, look,' she began to say nervously. 'I've been thinking whether or not I should do this and, um . . .'

Specky caught himself looking at Tiger Girl.

Wow, she really does have a cute nose. And her eyes are really green . . . Why haven't I noticed any of this before? Maybe Dieter's right. Christina won't even talk to me.

'Um, I know it's gonna take you by surprise,' Tiger Girl continued. 'But . . .'

Specky glanced back at the Great McCarthy. He was deliberately looking in their direction, which made Specky feel extra uncomfortable. He looked toward the kitchen. Thankfully there were no parents in sight.

This is it, he thought. Oh, man, how am I going to do this? How do you make the first move? I should've been paying more attention to that James Bond movie I watched last week. I think my breath stinks. I should have brought chewy with me.

Suddenly Specky leant forward and tried to kiss Tiger Girl.

'What the . . . ?' she squealed, pushing him back.

Specky was completely shocked. Not by Tiger Girl's reaction, but because of the person standing at the open front door.

'Christina!' gulped Specky, as she turned and ran back out to her dad in the car. 'What is she doing here?'

'That's the surprise, you goose! I invited her to come and stay the night,' exclaimed Tiger Girl, rushing out the door after her.

Specky couldn't believe it – talk about feeling like a complete loser. He turned and saw the Great McCarthy wincing and looking apologetic.

Tiger Girl returned a few minutes later – without Christina.

'Well, she's gone. She didn't want to hang around,' she puffed. 'She thought we were an item. And I tried to convince her we weren't, which was really humiliating to say in front of her dad. Why did you have to go and kiss me? What were you thinking?'

'Um, I thought, that, um,' stuttered Specky. 'I thought the surprise was that *you* were gonna kiss *me*.'

'What? Where d'ya get that crazy idea from?'

Specky glared back at the Great McCarthy.

Tiger Girl followed his gaze and then looked back at Specky.

'Right. I get it,' she said, annoyed. 'It's McCarthy's fault . . . Speck, we're mates,' she continued in a softer voice. 'You're like a brother to me. And even if I did like you that way, I wouldn't chase ya, 'cause I know how much Christina means to you.'

Specky shook his head, upset that he had allowed himself to be pressured by Dieter.

'Besides,' said Tiger Girl, 'I thought you were gonna do something to show Christina how much you care?'

'I was. I am. I had it under control! So why did you have to go and invite her without telling me?' replied Specky, turning it back on Tiger Girl.

''Cause I thought you could talk, just in case whatever you were planning didn't work out. She knew you'd be here and she still came, didn't she?'

This was getting too complicated for Specky. Trying to understand girls was tough work.

After the party, Specky went home knowing one thing. It was going to be doubly hard for him to impress Christina and get her to like him again. With that in mind, he knew what he had to do the next morning.

18. emotional rival

'Excuse me. Mr Li?'

'Yes?' replied Screamer's piano tutor, smiling warmly. 'How can I help you?'

Specky knew there was no way Screamer would agree to sit the audition if it clashed with the footy game – he had to find out more details.

'The audition?' said Mr Li. 'It will be held on the eighth, next Sunday, at the Victorian College of the Arts on St Kilda Road. Derek's pencilled in for ten-thirty in the morning.'

It's two hours before the State selection match, thought Specky.

'I very much hope Derek will make it through,' added Mr Li. 'He is lucky to have a friend like you who supports him. Are you a musical friend or one of his football friends?'

Specky coughed nervously, feeling a little guilty to be calling himself one of Screamer's friends.

'I play footy with him,' he replied.

'One should never ignore their true passion,' Mr Li went on. 'Passion feeds the soul. Derek's soul is fed every time he plays the piano. He is very lucky to have so much potential. And I hope he comes to realise that before it's too late. But very talented people sometimes have to make very difficult choices.'

For a moment, Specky pondered what Mr Li was saying – maybe Screamer *would* have to choose between piano and football, but he didn't have to choose yet.

'Well, thanks for your time,' he said, standing up.

'You're not staying? Derek should be here soon for his lesson. I'm sure he'd be happy to have you sit in.'

Yeah, right, if only you knew, thought Specky.

'No, thanks, Mr Li. I gotta get going.'

And with that Specky made his way out of the building, only to run straight into Screamer outside.

'What the hell are you doing here?' he growled.

Specky froze, but he realised this was probably his only opportunity to talk to Screamer. He took a deep breath and launched straight into it.

'I think you should do that audition,' he said quickly. 'Mr Li thinks you have a real good chance. I know it's on the same day as the State trial game, but you can do the audition and still make it to the match in time.'

'What's it to you if I do or I don't, Magee?' Screamer replied, stone-faced.

'I just think you should, that's all.'

'Bull!' snapped Screamer, taking a few steps toward Specky. 'You don't care what I do. What's the real reason?'

'What?' asked Specky, as if he had no idea what Screamer was talking about.

'Enough of the good-guy act, Magee! Tell me what the hell you're up to.'

With Christina on his mind, Specky was surprised at the answer that suddenly popped into his head.

'Look, um, the truth is that I came here this morning to convince you to do this audition for

Christina – she's the one that cares if you play piano or not. But then I realised that it's not just that. That's not what's important.' Specky was stuttering now, trying to find the right words. 'What's important is that everyone, including you, deserves a fair go. Everyone deserves to go after their dreams and not just do things to make other people happy.'

Screamer shook his head, biting his bottom lip. 'You're pathetic, Magee!' he snarled, brushing past Specky. 'Just keep your big nose out of my life.'

Screamer walked up the steps into the building, his back toward Specky.

'I know about your brother, Craig,' Specky blurted out.

Screamer stopped at the top step and slowly turned to face him.

'I'm sorry you lost him,' Specky said hastily. 'I know that he was a gun footballer – a legend in the making.'

Screamer deliberately stomped down each step until he got to Specky.

'How d'ya find out?' he hissed.

'I saw you at the cemetery, on the day of

Danny's grandmother's funeral. I saw your brother's grave. I wasn't sure if I should talk to ya about it or not. And don't worry, I haven't told anyone.'

Screamer moved closer to Specky. His eyes were dark and cold. Specky clenched his fists, ready to defend himself, just in case.

'How'd he die?' asked Specky, knowing it probably wasn't the best thing to ask.

Screamer stood still and stared.

'Was it some sort of accident?' croaked Specky, uncomfortably.

Screamer still didn't respond.

'Look, I'm sorry for you, mate. I don't know what I'd do if I were in your situation. And I know the pressure you get from your old man, but –'

'He was hit by a car.'

Specky stopped talking.

'He was playing footy with his friends. Not a game. Just kick-to-kick,' Screamer said, his voice beginning to crack. 'I, um, I . . .'

He took a deep breath.

'I was running over to him to see if I could join in and one of his mates kicked the ball over his head onto the road. As Craig ran for it, I called out to him.'

Screamer's eyes began to well with tears. He quickly wiped them away with the back of his sleeve.

'He didn't see the car. I didn't see it. If I hadn't called out to him and distracted him, he might've seen it.'

Screamer dropped his head and sniffed. Specky wasn't sure what to say. Screamer took a few minutes to compose himself.

'What did ya mean about the pressure I get from my old man?' Screamer asked, raising his head, his eyes red.

'I heard your mum say that you're not Craig and . . .' Specky stopped, wondering whether he should go on or not.

'And what?' pushed Screamer.

'And, well, I think even though you love your footy, maybe you'd rather be a musician, but maybe you feel pressure to be like your brother to make your dad happy. Maybe you feel a little bit guilty, too.'

Specky thought he probably sounded like that Dr Phil guy from the TV, but he had only said what he believed to be true. In all the time he had known Screamer, he had never understood why he was the way he was until this very moment.

'So, maybe you've got to start thinking about what *you* want,' Specky added quickly, noticing Screamer's face hardening again. 'So, do the audition. Not for your dad or your mum or even for Craig. Do it for yourself.'

'Derek!'

It was Mr Li gesturing for Screamer to come inside.

Specky waited for Screamer to say something, but he didn't. He just turned and headed into the building.

19. state trial

Mr Magee and Specky pulled up outside Princes Park, the home of the Carlton Football Club. There was already a big crowd heading into the ground, made up mostly of the family and friends of the forty boys who were hoping to make the Victorian side.

Everyone was aware that all the recruiting officers of the AFL clubs would be in attendance, as well. Although most of these boys were only 14, the reality was that some of them were only three years away from being eligible to be selected in the national draft. A lot could happen in the space of three years, but there was no doubt that the recruiting officers would leave today's trial game with more than a couple of names jotted down in their little black books for future reference. This just added to the sense of excitement and anticipation.

As Specky entered the change rooms the first thing he noticed were the photos hung on the walls of the club rooms. All of the legends of the Carlton Football Club were honoured with action shots from their playing days. There was John Nicholls, the captain of their team of the century, and Alex Jesaulenko, taking one of the most famous specky-marks of all time in the 1970 Grand Final. There were pictures of Stephen Kernahan, Steven Silvagni, Greg Williams and Craig Bradley, four of the greatest players of the modern era.

'Pretty cool, huh?'

It was Brian Edwards. He walked alongside Specky, every bit as awe-struck about being there as Specky was.

'You know, I barrack for the Mighty Blues,' Brian said proudly. 'Greg Williams was unbelievable. I've got seventeen video tapes at home of his best games. He's the player I've tried to base my game on. If I could be one hundredth of the player he was, I'd be happy.'

'Yeah, he was awesome,' agreed Specky.

'How ya feeling?' Brian asked.

'I'm nervous as hell,' replied Specky.

'Try to think of it as just another game of footy. That's what I'm doing. It's probably the most important game I've ever played in, but it's still just a game,' shrugged Brian.

Specky marvelled at how cool and calm Brian was as they walked to the lockers and put their bags away.

'Don't get changed next to him, boy!' Mr Johnson motioned Screamer to choose another locker not so close to Specky. 'Get over the other side of the room.'

Specky pulled a face. He noticed Screamer was doing his best not to make eye contact. Specky wondered how he had gone at the audition – whether he had even turned up.

There's no way he's gonna tell me, not with his old man right by his side all the time, Specky thought. Besides, there's nothing else I can do. It's up to him now. His life is his life.

'Righto, you guys!' bellowed Grub Gordan, marching into the rooms. 'You can start to get changed. We've picked two teams and they're written up on the whiteboard in the coaches' room. One team will wear blue jumpers and the other will wear white. The Blue team will stay here with Evan Dillon and the white team will go next door with Bob Stockdale.'

Evan Dillon and Bob Stockdale stepped up beside Grub Gordan.

'I'll float between both sides,' he continued. 'But I want to be able to sit back and have a good look at all of you, so these guys will be in charge for the day. Now, off you go. There will be a team meeting in thirty minutes.'

All of the boys rushed to the coaches' room to find out where they were playing. Specky frantically searched for his name and finally found it. He had been named on the half-forward flank for the White team.

Screamer was in the forward pocket and, much to Specky's delight, Brian Edwards had been picked in the centre on the same team.

'Looks like I'll be putting a few Sherrins down your throat today, Simon,' said Brian.

'Well, you pass 'em and I'll grab 'em,' answered Specky, pleased that he would have at least one familiar face in his side, other than Screamer's.

'And, by the way, no one calls me Simon. Just Specky will do.'

'Specky, huh?' Brian replied. 'That's cool. I like it. I hope you can live up to your nickname, Specky.'

Once the boys had changed into their gear and laced up their boots, Grub Gordan called them into the coaches' room.

'Boys, I'm not going to take much of your time here,' he said, with the sound of the ice machine buzzing faintly behind him. 'I know some of you are probably nervous and just want to get out there and play, and that's fair enough. The only thing I want to say is that we are not just looking for the *best* players today. We are looking for the players that can best fit into a team. You may think you have to be one of the best on ground to make the final squad. Take it from me, that's not the case. In fact, if you are best on ground, but you're only playing for yourself and not working with the rest of the team, then the chances are very good that you *won't* be picked. Do the best you can, but always bear that in mind. I see it all the time in representative sides. Don't be tempted to play for yourself. Good luck and enjoy yourselves.'

As Grub left the room, Specky and the other players made their way out on to the ground for the biggest test of their young football lives.

Specky jogged out to his position on the half-forward flank. He had noticed, as they did their warm-up lap, that not only were his parents there to cheer him on, but so, it seemed, were half of Booyong High.

Johnny, Robbo, Danny, the Bombay Bullet, Gobba and Smashing Sols were sitting with Alice and the Great McCarthy. Coach Pate was there as well. He also noticed Tiger Girl in the crowd with some of her friends. She had forgiven him for what had happened at the party and they'd shared a few jokes about it. The only person missing was Christina.

Before the ball was bounced, the runner dashed out to Specky from the boundary.

'Magee, Grub said to swap to the other half-forward flank, and to start up on the side of the centre square a bit. As the ball is bounced, he wants you to run hard into the middle, and if you get possession, you'll then be able to kick the ball straight away on your preferred foot. The other half-forward flanker is a left footer, so it makes sense to swap sides.'

Specky did as the runner told him and swapped places with a solid left-footer from Wonthaggi who answered to the name Gomez.

Gee, that makes sense, Specky thought. Why didn't I think of that?

The ball was bounced and Specky sprinted into the square just as Grub had instructed.

The 195 centimetre ruckman, a kid called 'Lurch' Freeman from Sunbury, punched the ball forward, right into Specky's path. Specky picked it up in one smooth motion and without having to change direction, swung onto his right foot. When he looked up the ground, the first face he saw was Screamer Johnson's. He was in the clear and leading straight at him.

Specky didn't hesitate. He speared a beautiful drop punt right onto the chest of his Booyong High teammate who marked easily, not giving his opponent any chance to spoil.

Loud cheering broke out from the section

of the crowd that contained the Booyong High faithful and Specky's family.

As Screamer went back and kicked the first goal of the game, Brian Edwards jogged past Specky, giving him a high five.

'You take Speckies *and* pass the ball. Great work, mate!'

'Thanks.' Specky smiled broadly.

The game went on to be a fantastic exhibition of junior football. The scores didn't matter at all, as all of the skills were on display. Grub Gordan roamed along the boundary lines, shouting out instructions at the top of his raspy voice. Most of it was criticism, but all of it was relevant and constructive.

Specky didn't slack off for one moment. He was having a good game without being spectacular. He had taken notice of what Grub had said before the match and focussed on working really hard on the defensive side of his game.

The only time he was questioned by Grub was when he took one of his big speckies. The fullback had kicked the ball in, and it was heading in Specky's direction. He had a perfect run at the ball and leapt on top of the two competing ruckman and pulled in a magnificent mark. The crowd went berserk as he fell to the ground.

Feeling pretty good about himself he jogged into the quarter-time huddle.

'Nice mark, Magee,' commented Grub. 'But did you realise that you had two of your team-mates at the front of the pack waiting for the crumbs?'

'Um,' stuttered Specky, caught off-guard by Grub's question.

'They saw that you were behind and antici-pated that you would have done the disciplined thing and punched the ball to the ground where they could have picked it up and run into an open goal. As it was, by the time you got your-self up off the ground, everyone was manned up, and all you could do was boot it back to a big pack at the top of the square.'

Specky wasn't sure what to say. Grub was dead right.

'Don't get me wrong,' Grub added. 'It was a great mark, but if you're going to go for them, by hell, you better grab them. If you had dropped it, I would have dragged you.'

Specky maintained eye contact with his coach,

confused whether he was actually criticising or praising him – or both. But before he had time to let it all sink in, Grub spoke again.

'But you are the leading tackler on the ground so far, with six for the quarter, and that's better than any specky you might take.'

Specky let out a huge sigh of relief as Grub turned his attention to another player.

'What do you think ya doin', Derek?'

It was Mr Johnson getting stuck into Screamer. Specky watched as Screamer swigged down some water.

'You're gonna blow this if you don't start kicking straight,' Screamer's dad growled.

Screamer didn't answer his father, but hung his head in shame.

'Hey, mister!' Grub called out to Mr Johnson.

Woah, this should be good, thought Specky.

'Would you mind getting away from the players and letting them get some rest?'

'What?' Screamer's dad snapped back.

'You heard me,' said Grub, not backing down.

'I can talk to my son any time I –' started Mr Johnson.

'Now, you listen to me, and listen good,'

interjected Grub. 'Your boy has got some ability, but you're his biggest obstacle, pal. And the sooner you realise it the better. I've been coaching junior footballers for longer than you've been adding up and I've seen all types of parents. Don't you even think about putting a foot inside that change room over there, unless you're happy to sit quietly in the corner and not say a word. Let your young bloke play football without having to worry about you embarrassing him. You got it?'

Specky looked around to see all eyes were now on Grub and Mr Johnson. He also noticed Screamer looking the most embarrassed he had ever seen him. Again, Specky felt for him.

'Yeah, all right,' mumbled Mr Johnson.

Specky couldn't believe it. Screamer's dad, who was so much bigger than Grub, had backed off. Within minutes everyone got back to focussing on the game as if it had never happened.

Once the third quarter got started, the match continued on a similar pattern to the first half, with one exception – Brian Edwards. He totally took over the game – clocking up seventeen possessions and kicking three goals for the quarter.

He was head and shoulders above every other player on the ground. His skills were outstanding and his courage took everyone's breath away.

Bob Stockdale approached Specky at the huddle before the last quarter and informed him that he wanted to see how he performed at full-forward. Specky could hardly contain his excitement. He had played a solid game and worked hard, but at this level, against players of equal ability, it was really tough playing in a position that he wasn't one hundred per cent used to. He was thrilled to get this opportunity to play in his favourite position and it meant he would have a chance to really shine.

As he jogged from the huddle, Brian Edwards called him over.

'If I get the ball, start your lead toward the boundary,' he said. 'I'll act as if I'm going to kick it there, but I'll always bring it back into the centre corridor. You just need to double back on your opponent and I'll make sure the ball is there for you.'

Specky nodded. He was still a bit awe-struck, after Brian's amazing third quarter and was determined not to let him down.

For the first few minutes of the final quarter, the Blue team dominated early possession. But suddenly the football was booted out to the wing and directly to Brian Edwards.

Brian picked it up and raced forward, taking a bounce in the process. At just the right moment, Specky led hard to the boundary line. The full-back anticipated this and raced two metres ahead of him.

With perfect timing, Specky quickly doubled back and sprinted to the middle of the ground, just as Brian dropped the ball onto his boot. For a moment, Specky thought it had all gone terribly wrong. Was Brian really going to kick it to the boundary? But at the last second, Brian swung his boot across his body and drilled the ball toward Specky.

Everyone, except the two of them, had been fooled – leaving Specky alone, ten metres in the clear.

He watched the ball come toward him, and with no one in sight he thought, to be safe, he should take a nice easy chest mark. But the words of Grub Gordan came ringing back to him.

Specky stretched out his arms and took a perfect, solid mark, out in front, *in his hands.*

'Four goals in a quarter! Good effort, Magee,' beamed Grub, standing alongside Specky and Brian as they enjoyed a sports drink after the game.

'Are you sure you two haven't played together before?' he asked. 'Maybe in primary school or something? The way you combined out there today was uncanny. It seemed like you could read each other's minds.'

Specky and Brian just shrugged and grinned at one another.

On the way home, slumped exhausted in the back seat of his dad's car, Specky hoped he had done enough. If he had been selected in the final State team, he was to expect a phone call within the next forty-eight hours.

All he had to do now was wait.

20. true passion

On the following Tuesday morning, Specky and the rest of the students of Booyong High streamed into the school hall for an assembly.

Mr and Mrs Magee made their way past the students toward the front row, and sat down with Coach Pate and some of the other teachers. A few moments later, Screamer's parents showed up and were also directed to the front row.

'Hey, what are your folks doing here?' asked Tiger Girl, pointing to the front of the hall.

'Yeah, um, Coach Pate is going to make an announcement about whether Screamer and I made the State team. She's asked us both to say a few words about it.'

'Seriously?' Johnny piped up. 'Does that mean you're in?'

'C'mon, Speck!' said Danny. 'You can tell us.'

'Why didn't ya say they were gonna announce it today?' asked Robbo.

''Cause I wasn't really sure myself. They only rang last night. And I wasn't allowed to say whether we got in or not anyway. Coach Pate said it's a part of the school's new thing to push students to develop their public speaking skills or something. They're gonna try to do it at every assembly. That's why the olds were invited. No big deal.' Specky shrugged modestly.

As Specky took his seat with his classmates, he glanced down his row at Screamer. Screamer acknowledged him with a nervous look. They certainly weren't friends now, but since they had talked on the steps of Mr Li's office there seemed to be an uneasy truce between them.

'Right, settle down everyone,' ordered Mr Radcliff, the Principal. 'There's a lot for us to get through this morning. But before we start, I'd like to call Miss Pate to the stage, please.'

Coach Pate stepped onto the stage and took the microphone from Mr Radcliff.

'Well,' she said. 'Today's a special assembly, because last Sunday two Booyong High Students tried out for the Victorian Under Fifteen football side that will be playing in the National Championships in September. In the final trial match played at Princes Park they both acquitted themselves very well. As you can all appreciate, this is an extremely difficult team to make and competition for places was incredibly challenging. After what I'm sure was a very nervous and anxious wait they received phone calls last night from the legendary junior football coach, Mr Jay Gordan. I am absolutely over the moon to announce that they have both been selected to represent Victoria in the National Carnival in Adelaide. As I call for them to join me on stage, could you please give them a huge clap and show them how very proud we are of them. Simon Magee and Derek Johnson!'

The hall erupted into cheers and applause. As the two boys made their way to the stage, Specky whispered in Screamer's direction.

'Look what's on stage.'

Screamer looked up. On the far righthand corner of the stage stood a piano. The same piano Shirley had used during deb practice.

'Yeah, so what?' said Screamer.

'Just saying, that's all.'

When the cheers died down, Coach Pate handed Specky the microphone first.

Specky took a deep breath. He looked down to the front row and saw his parents smiling proudly at him.

'Um, on Sunday, Screamer, I mean, Derek, and I had the opportunity to try out for the Victorian Schoolboys football side . . .'

Specky went on to review the match.

'. . . and, finally, I want to thank all my team-mates, school friends and family who came to the ground to support us. And that's it. Thank you.'

Everyone applauded. As Coach Pate moved to take the microphone, Specky quickly turned back to the audience.

'Um, there's something else I wanted to say.' Specky looked to Coach Pate for permission, and she nodded.

'I've been really lucky that I've been able to do what I love most, which is play footy. 'Cause I know a lot of people don't get that chance.'

Specky shot a quick glance at Screamer.

'Some of us are also lucky to be talented at a couple of different things. Like Shane Warne was good at footy as well as cricket when he was our age. And everyone knows that Michael Jordan played baseball for a year after quitting basketball for a while. But in the end, they had to choose what they were most passionate about. They had to be true to themselves. It's easy for me – I only have one true passion and that's footy, but I wanted to thank my parents for supporting me and letting me do what I love so much.'

Mrs Magee took Mr Magee's hand and beamed with pride.

'I also want to thank Derek Johnson.'

Specky turned to see Screamer looking surprised, and a little suspicious.

'He helped me realise that when you're lucky enough to be good at something that you're passionate about, then no one should stop you from doing it. So, thanks, mate, and thank you, Coach Pate.'

The hall echoed loudly with applause as Specky returned the microphone to Coach Pate.

'Thank you, Simon, for those inspiring words,'

smiled Coach Pate. 'Right, now, Derek, a few words from you.'

Screamer took the microphone.

'Um,' he said, coughing nervously. 'We had a good game on Sunday and I'd like to thank my parents, too. Thanks.'

Screamer turned to give the mic back to Coach Pate.

'That's it?' she whispered to Screamer.

'Yeah.' Screamer nodded.

'Okay, then,' said Coach Pate, taking back the microphone.

'No, no, wait,' said Screamer, reaching for the microphone again.

Coach Pate joked that it was like playing a game of Pass-the-Parcel, but she gladly handed it back to Screamer.

'Um, I just want to say – it's true, you know,' croaked Screamer. 'Everything Magee, I mean Simon, said about picking what you're really passionate about and then going for it. It's all true.'

Screamer paused. He dropped his head for a moment. Murmurs rippled through the hall.

'What's he doing?'

'Is he all right?'

'He looks upset!'

'Um, Dad,' Screamer raised his head, now looking down at his parents. 'Remember, on the morning of the game you got mad with me 'cause you asked where I had disappeared to. Well, I went to an audition. And I did really well. So well, that I got in.'

Yes! thought Specky, smiling, and catching Mr Johnson turning to Mrs Johnson with a confused look. Screamer continued.

'I love footy, Dad. But the truth is that the main reason I play it is so you can be proud of me – the same way you were with Craig.'

Specky again looked down at Screamer's parents. His father squirmed in his chair. His mother appeared close to tears. Coach Pate, Mr Radcliff and everyone else looked totally baffled.

'But I want you to be proud of me for who *I* am, not because I remind you of Craig. 'Cause I don't want to be like Craig anymore. I wanna be me. I'm sorry, Dad. I love footy, but I love this more . . .'

Screamer walked over to the piano, opened the lid and placed the mic on top.

Some of the students at the back of the hall got out of their chairs to get a better look. Specky caught Tiger Girl, Danny, Robbo, Johnny, and his classmates shooting him a look as if to say, 'What's going on?'

Screamer sat down at the piano and started to play. There were gasps of shock from everyone. Mr Johnson's expression was impossible to read.

It was hard to believe that this magnificent music was being performed by a boy that most of them knew, from personal experience or by reputation, to be a tough, in-your-face bully. Most people thought that Screamer was incapable of showing any emotion other than anger and bitterness.

As he played, it was obvious to everyone that Derek Johnson had a rare talent. He lost himself in the music as his fingers raced across the keys, making what should have been the most complicated piece of music look ridiculously easy. It was hauntingly beautiful.

As the music reached its crescendo, something happened to Screamer that Specky had not witnessed in all the time he had known him –

a smile came over his face. A real, genuine, soulful smile. The smile of someone who was truly happy.

When Screamer stopped, the hall erupted. It was pandemonium, and Specky had never witnessed cheering and applause like it. Not in this hall, not at a football game, not ever. It was spine tingling and he could feel the hairs stand up on the back of his neck. Everyone jumped to their feet and cheered wildly – including Specky. The only person not clapping was Mr Johnson.

Screamer stood by the piano, stunned by the standing ovation. As the applause died down, Mr Johnson stood up out of his seat stone-faced, his stare fixed on his son.

The entire school, including Coach Pate, Mr Radcliff and all the teachers had gone dead silent – waiting to see how Screamer's dad would react.

Mr Johnson marched to the steps leading up to the stage. He stopped and looked back at his wife, then made his way up on stage.

Specky watched intently. What was he going to do?

Mr Johnson moved toward Screamer. For a

moment, Specky could only think the worst. Screamer was going to be dragged off by his father, probably by the ear, and humiliated in front of everyone.

But suddenly, out of the blue, Mr Johnson opened up his arms and hugged Screamer tightly. Specky couldn't stop smiling. He looked down at his own dad who winked at him, then he saw Mrs Johnson smiling joyfully.

As the whoops and whistles continued to fill the Booyong School Hall, Specky caught Screamer, still in his father's embrace, raise his hand and give him the thumbs up. Specky nodded at his long-time rival and raised his thumb in return.

21. watch this space

'Hey, you're in *The Bugle* again,' Alice said, bursting into Specky's bedroom and throwing the school newspaper on his bed.

'Yeah, I knew I was gonna be in it this time,' said Specky, sitting at his desk doing some homework. 'Full On came up to me after –'

'You mean Theresa Fallon?'

'Yeah, Full On. She came to me yesterday after assembly – wanted to get a few quotes.'

'Cool!' said Alice. 'Well, you should check out the article she wrote. It's really good. And your friend Gobba's in the paper, too.'

'Gobba? What for?'

'There's an article about him getting a call from that footy commentator Dennis

Com . . . com . . . com . . .'

'Dennis Cometti?'

'Yeah. He invited Gobba to Perth for a week of training to be a sports commentator.'

'Ahh, that explains why he's been acting all weird, saying he's off on a trip that we'll all find out about soon,' Specky smiled. 'Nice one, Gobba!'

Ring, ring.

'I'll get it!'

Alice lunged forward to pick up the phone, but Specky got to it first.

'Hello?'

'Hi, Speck.'

It was Christina. Specky was speechless.

'Hi,' he just managed to choke out.

'Um, Speck,' she said. 'I heard about what happened at your assembly yesterday.'

'You did?'

'Yeah. And I know all about how you tried to help Screamer.'

'You do?'

'Yeah. He's just called me. And told me everything.'

Specky wasn't sure what to say. He was

recovering from the surprise of her call – but he didn't want to say the wrong thing again.

'Um, yeah, well . . .'

'Anyway, I'm heading to the movies now and I was just wondering if you'd like to catch up or go and see a film to celebrate you getting into the State team?'

'With you?' exclaimed Specky.

'Yeah, with me,' she replied. There was silence for a second. 'That's if you want to.'

Specky smiled.

'Yeah, yeah I do! I really do! Um, I'll see you soon then.'

Specky hung up the phone. He couldn't contain his excitement – everything was going to be okay for him and Christina.

Specky hurried out of the room without even bothering to read the article in the school newspaper.

A LEGEND IN THE MAKING

By Theresa Fallon

Those of us who witnessed yesterday's emotional school assembly involving Derek Johnson's surprise piano performance will remember it for a long, long time.

But yours truly will also remember the unsung hero that sparked off that moving moment – his name, Simon 'Specky' Magee.

After his awesome display at Sunday's State selection game, Magee has won many of us over once again. Not only did he make Booyong High proud to call him our own, the heartfelt remarks he made at yesterday's assembly about his love for the game can only make us admire him more.

When asked for further comments, he said, 'It's a dream of mine to one day play in the AFL and I'm never gonna give up on it. It's as simple as that.'

And we here at *The Bugle* have no argument.

Specky Magee, you are a legend – a real football legend in the making!

And to those of you who wonder if his dream will come true?

Well, then . . . WATCH THIS SPACE!

Also available from Puffin

Specky Magee and
the Great Footy Contest

Specky comes face to face with a tough, talented player by the name of Derek 'Screamer' Johnson, responsible for having him sent off during a game last season. The two boys become bitter rivals and when a popular TV show runs a nationwide football contest, Specky is relieved when everyone except Screamer decides to enter. But why is Screamer such a bully on the field? And why is he sucking up to Specky's team-mates? Specky's a true champion in the making, but is he good enough to win the Great Footy Contest?

Also available from Puffin

Specky Magee and
the Season of Champions

The Lions are playing well and Specky's form is looking good – perhaps good enough to win a scholarship to a prestigious sporting school. But when a knee injury sees him sidelined, suddenly his future is filled with uncertainty. Will the Booyong Lions make the finals without him? How can he impress the talent scout if he can't play? And who on earth is Tiger Girl? Specky soon discovers that there's more to being a champion than just being a legend on the field.

Also available from Puffin

Specky Magee and
the Boots of Glory

When Specky leaves his beloved Booyong High, he's torn between his old friends and his new team-mates. And his loyalty will be tested – on the field and off – because when he crosses that white line, Booyong becomes his enemy . . . And Gosmore Grammar expects nothing short of absolute loyalty from their new star student as Specky prepares to play a vital part in the school's most revered sporting event – the Boots of Glory football match. But will his need to solve a mystery at the school put his footy future in jeopardy?

COME EXPLORING AT

www.penguin.com.au

AND

www.puffin.com.au

FOR

Author and illustrator profiles

Book extracts

Reviews

Competitions

Activities, games and puzzles

Advice for budding authors

Tips for parents

Teacher resources